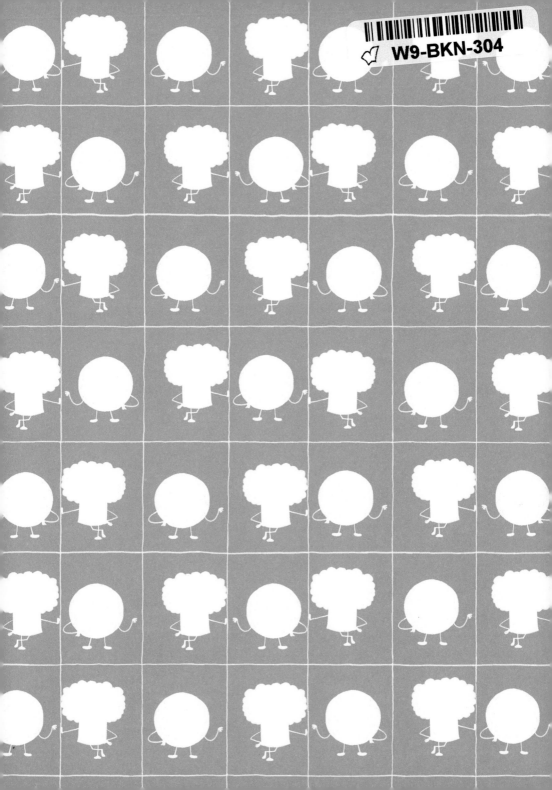

W9-BKN-304

COOKIE & BROCCOLI

PLAY IT COOL

Cool dance!

Cool face!

Bob McMahon

Dial Books for Young Readers

To Lalane, Tyler, and our dog Sam.
The coolest crowd I know.

DIAL BOOKS FOR YOUNG READERS

An imprint of Penguin Random House LLC, New York

First published in the United States of America by Dial Books for Young Readers,
an imprint of Penguin Random House LLC, 2021
Copyright © 2021 by Bob McMahon

Visit us online at penguinrandomhouse.com.

Library of Congress Cataloging-in-Publication Data is available.
Manufactured in China
ISBN 9780593109090

2   4   6   8   10   9   7   5   3   1

Design by Jennifer Kelly
Text handlettered by the author

This artwork was created digitally using Corel Painter
and by eating lots of barbeque potato chips.

CONTENTS

Chapter 1:
Are You Cool Enough for the Cool Crowd?
1

Chapter 2:
Broccoli Decides What Is Cool and What Is NOT!
31

Chapter 3:
Broccoli's Big Escape!
47

A Cookie and Broccoli Quiz: Are You Cool?
68

Epilogue
71

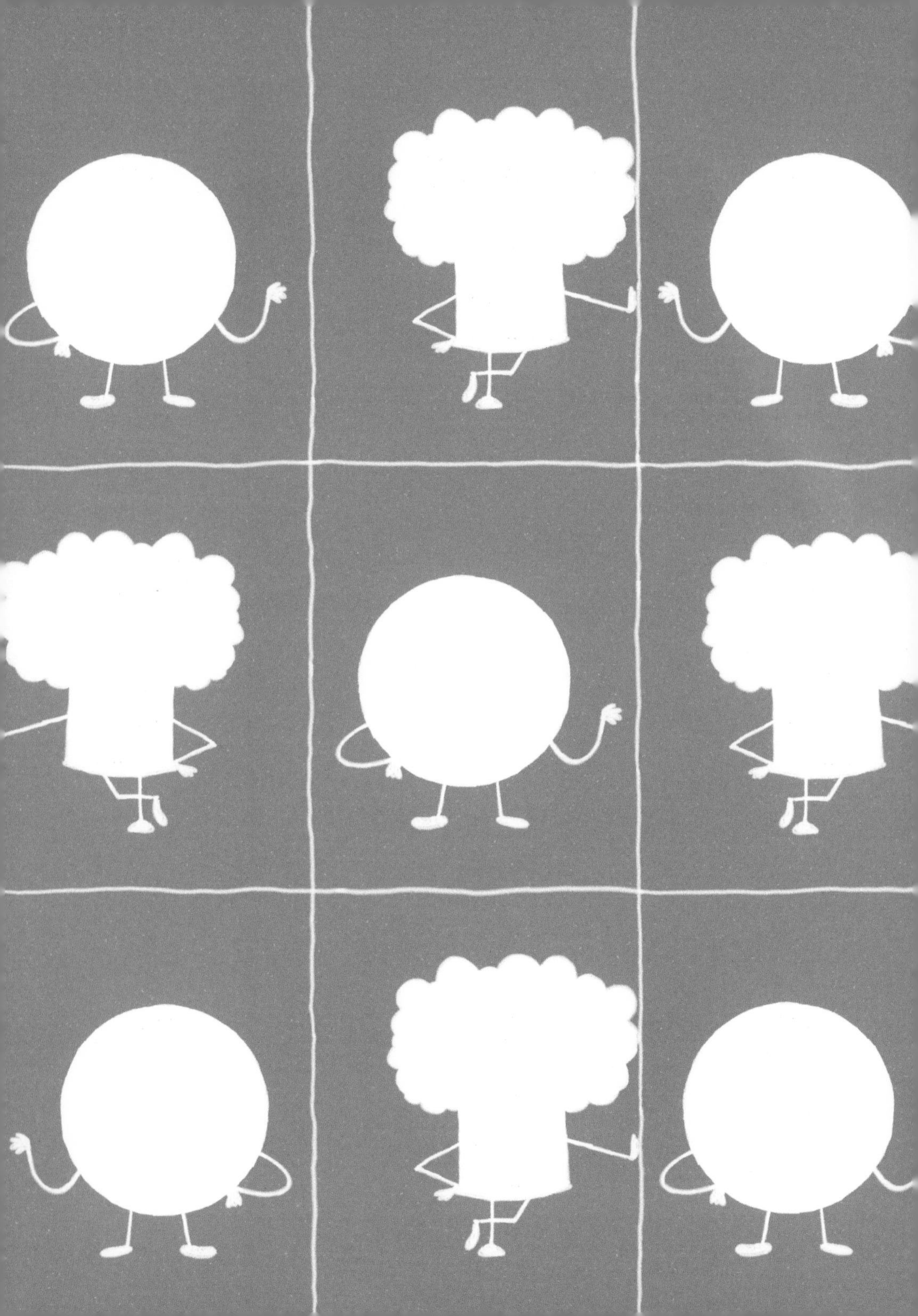

Chapter 1

ARE YOU COOL ENOUGH FOR THE COOL CROWD?

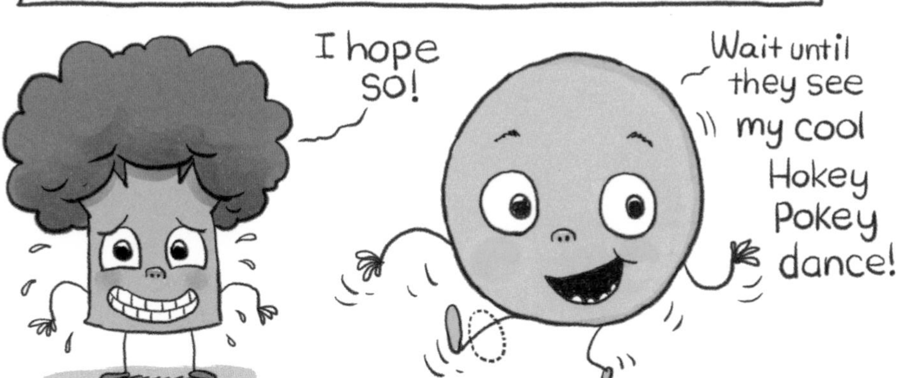
I hope so!
Wait until they see my cool Hokey Pokey dance!

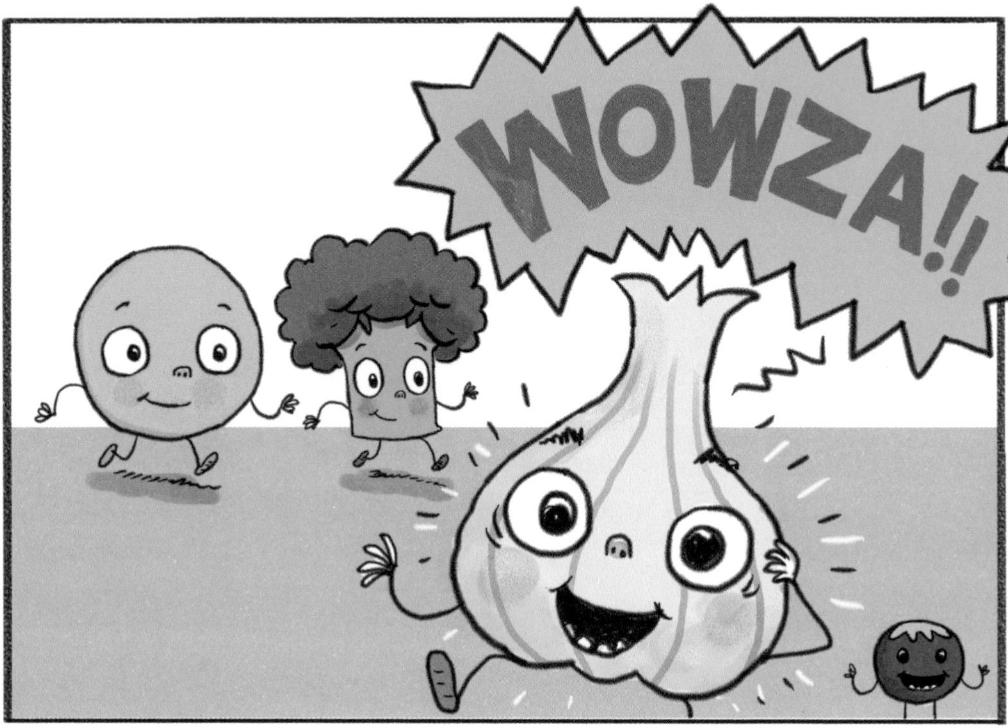
WOWZA!!

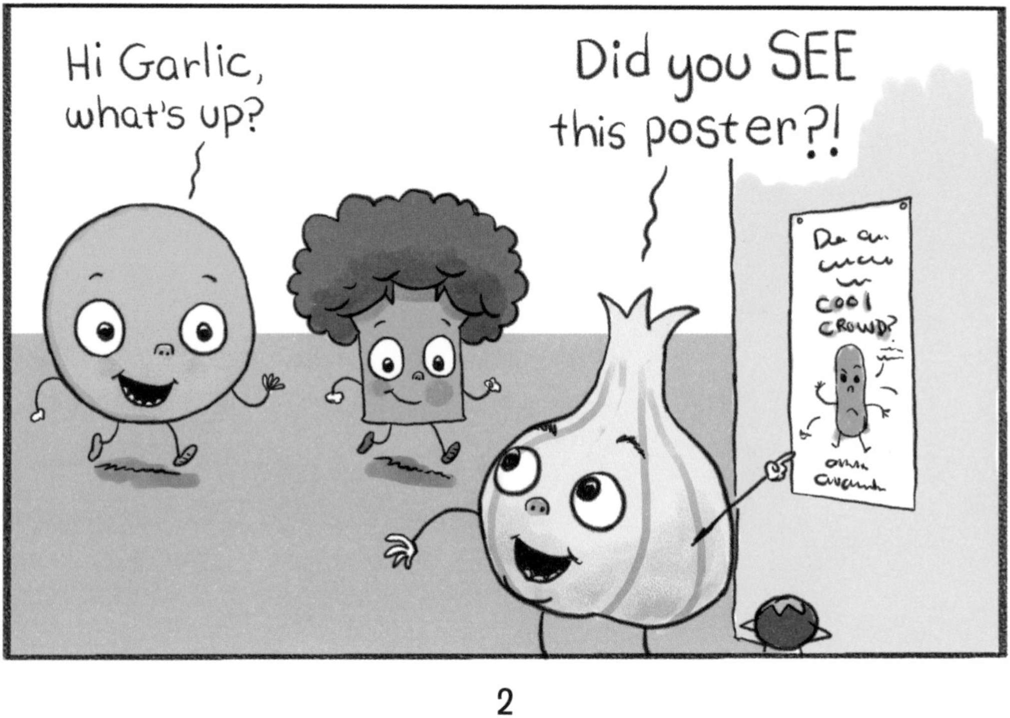
Hi Garlic, what's up?
Did you SEE this poster?!
COOL CROWD?

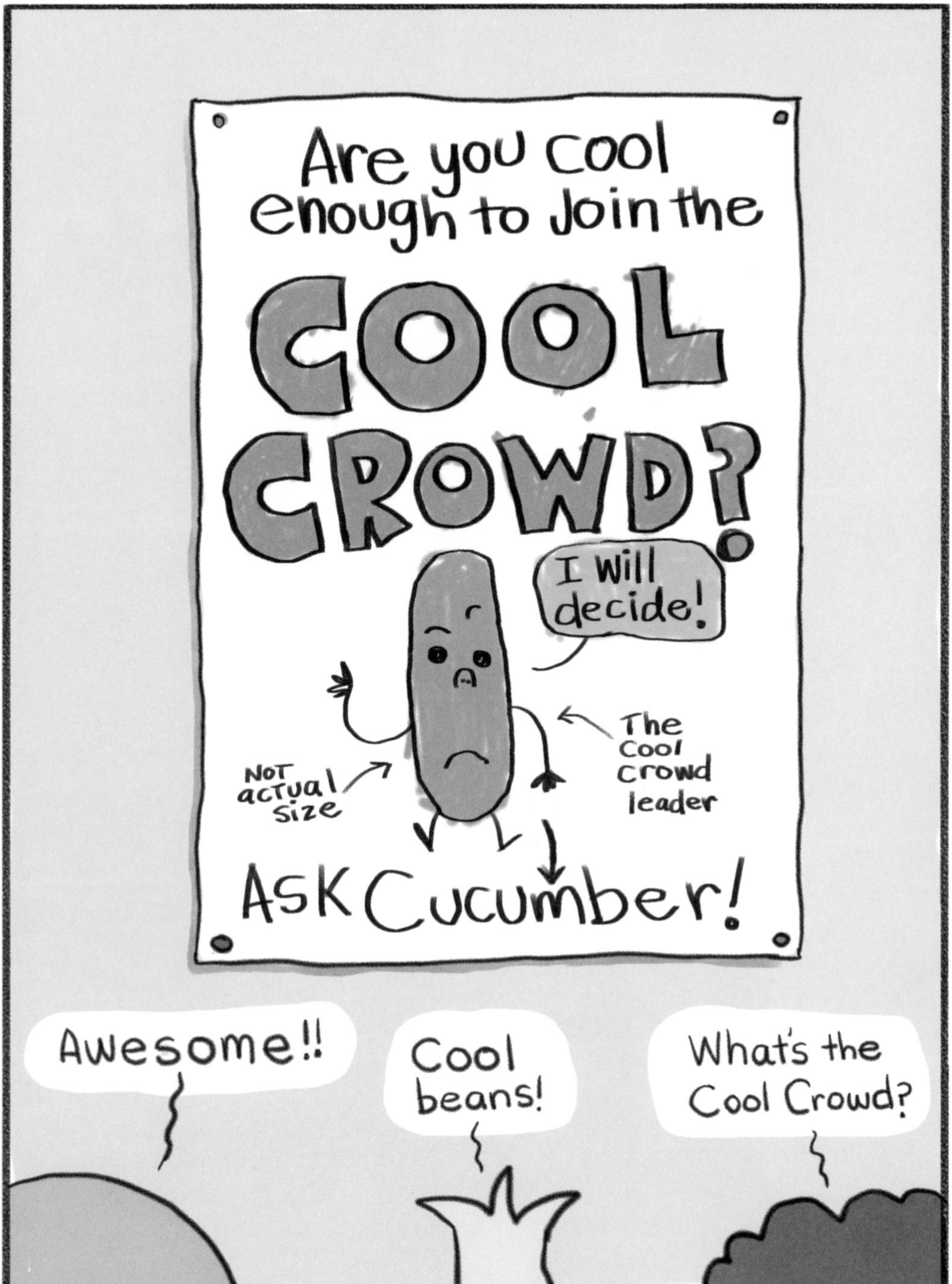
Are you cool enough to join the
COOL CROWD?
I will decide!
Not actual size
The cool crowd leader
ASK Cucumber!
Awesome!!
Cool beans!
What's the Cool Crowd?

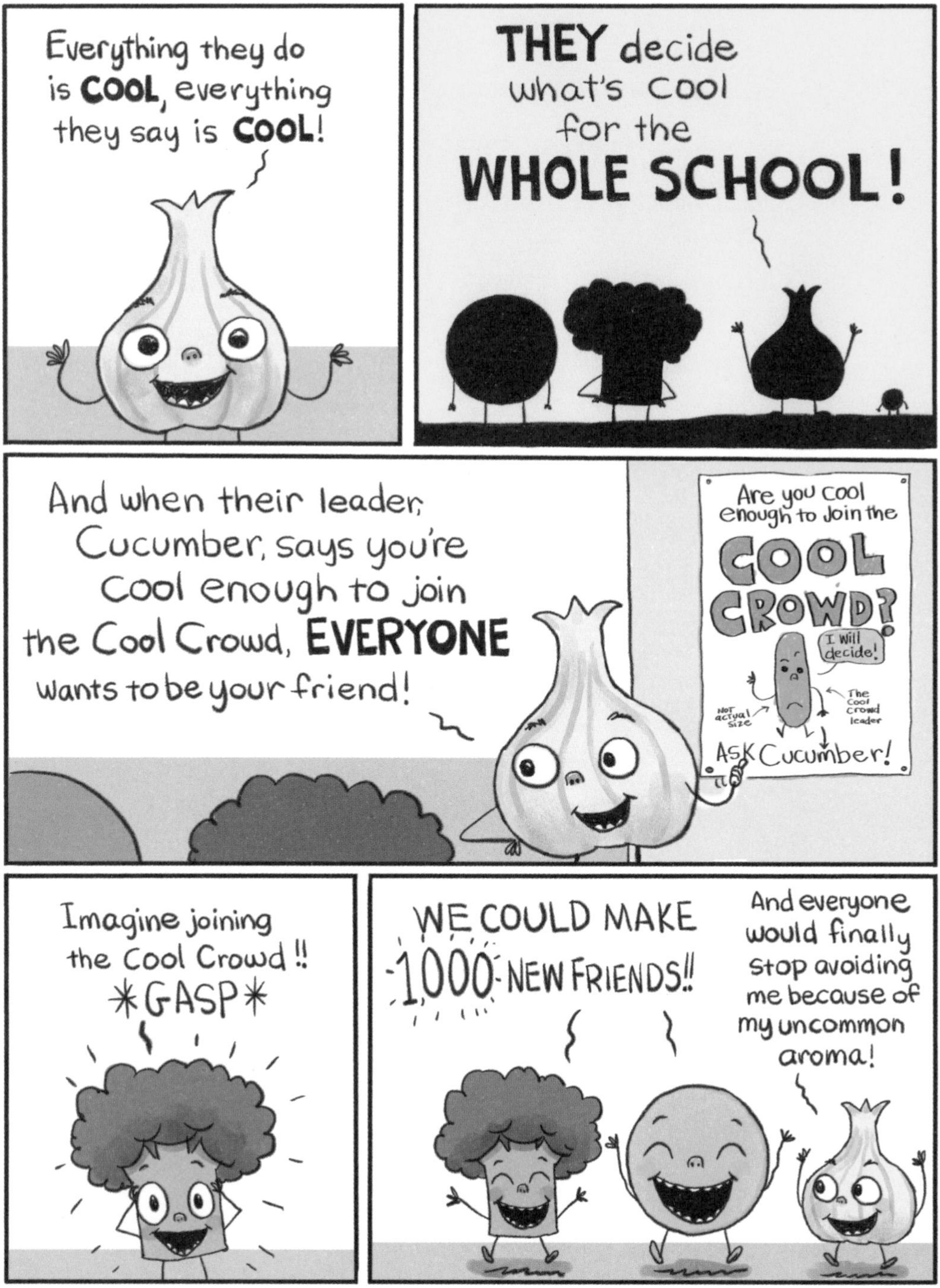
Everything they do is COOL, everything they say is COOL!
THEY decide what's cool for the WHOLE SCHOOL!
And when their leader, Cucumber, says you're cool enough to join the Cool Crowd, EVERYONE wants to be your friend!
Are you cool enough to Join the
COOL CROWD?
I Will decide!
The Cool Crowd leader
NOT actual size
ASK Cucumber!
Imagine joining the Cool Crowd!!
GASP
WE COULD MAKE 1,000 NEW FRIENDS!!
And everyone would finally stop avoiding me because of my uncommon aroma!

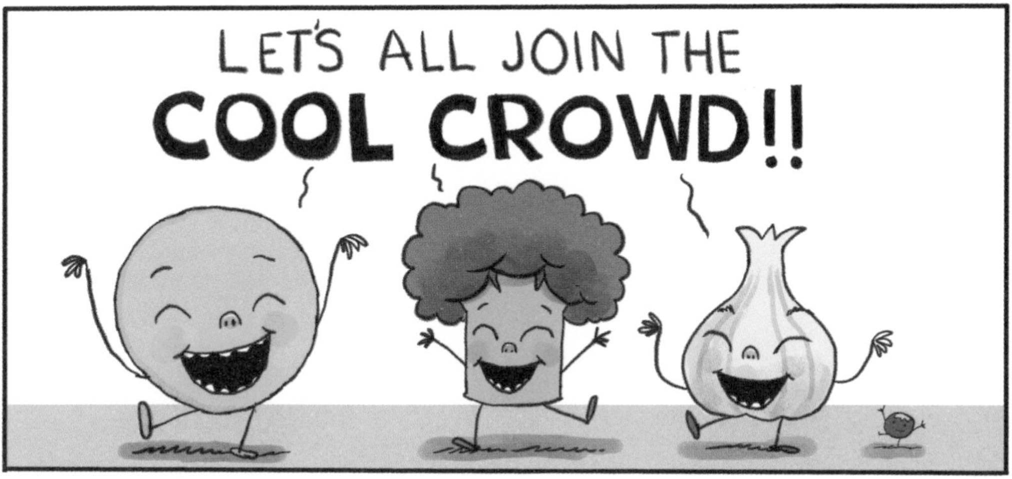
LET'S ALL JOIN THE
COOL CROWD!!

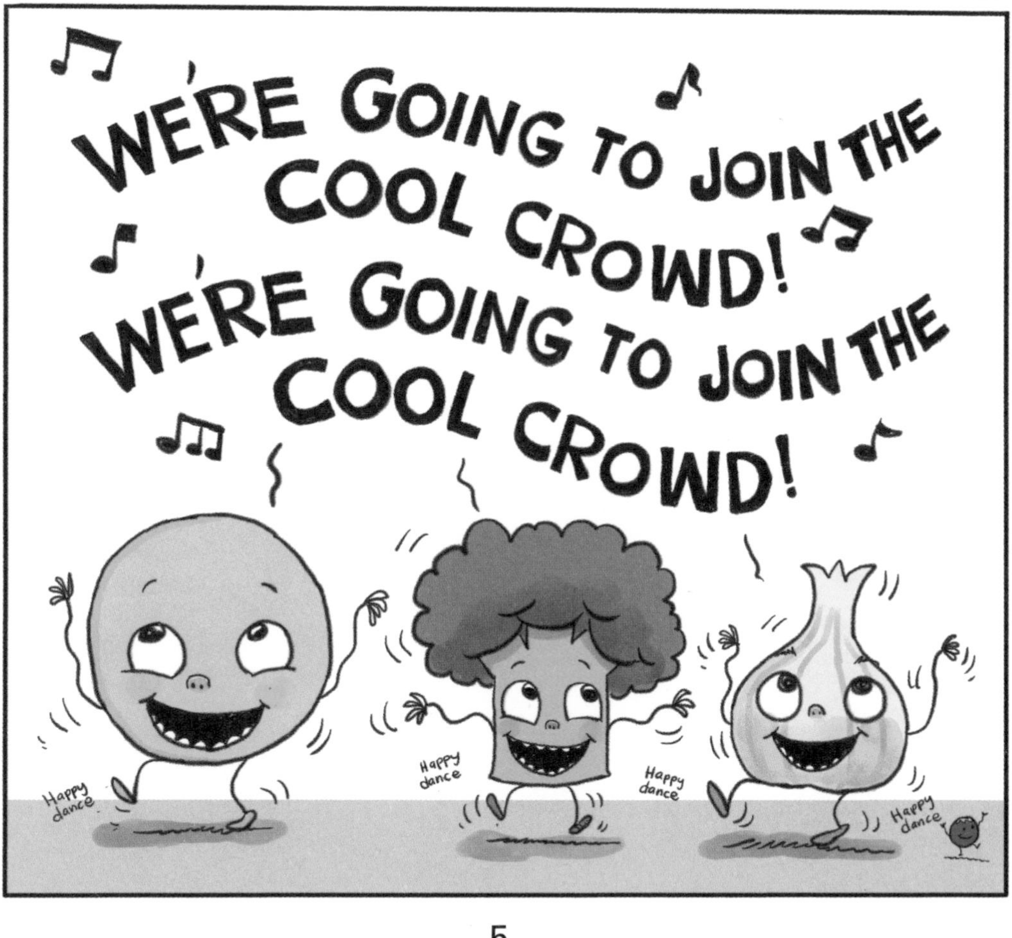
WE'RE GOING TO JOIN THE
COOL CROWD!
WE'RE GOING TO JOIN THE
COOL CROWD!
Happy dance
Happy dance
Happy dance
Happy dance

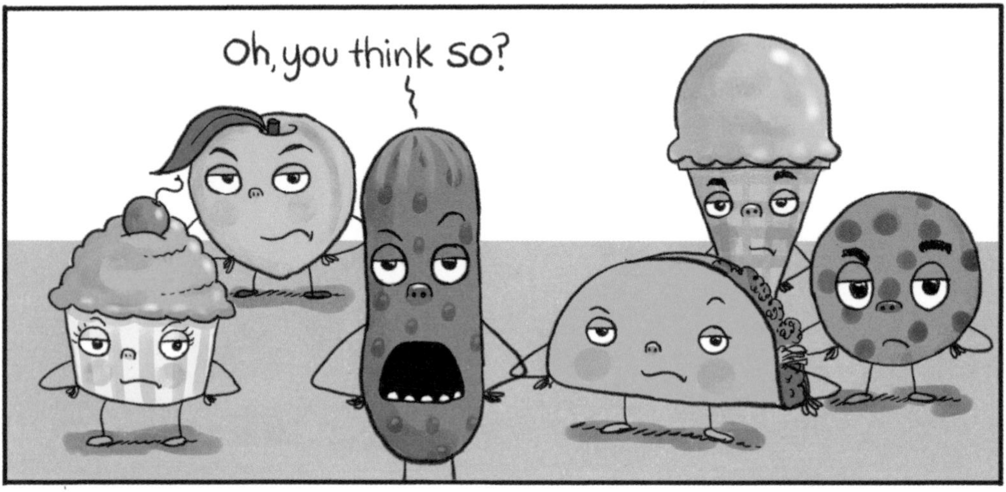
Oh, you think so?

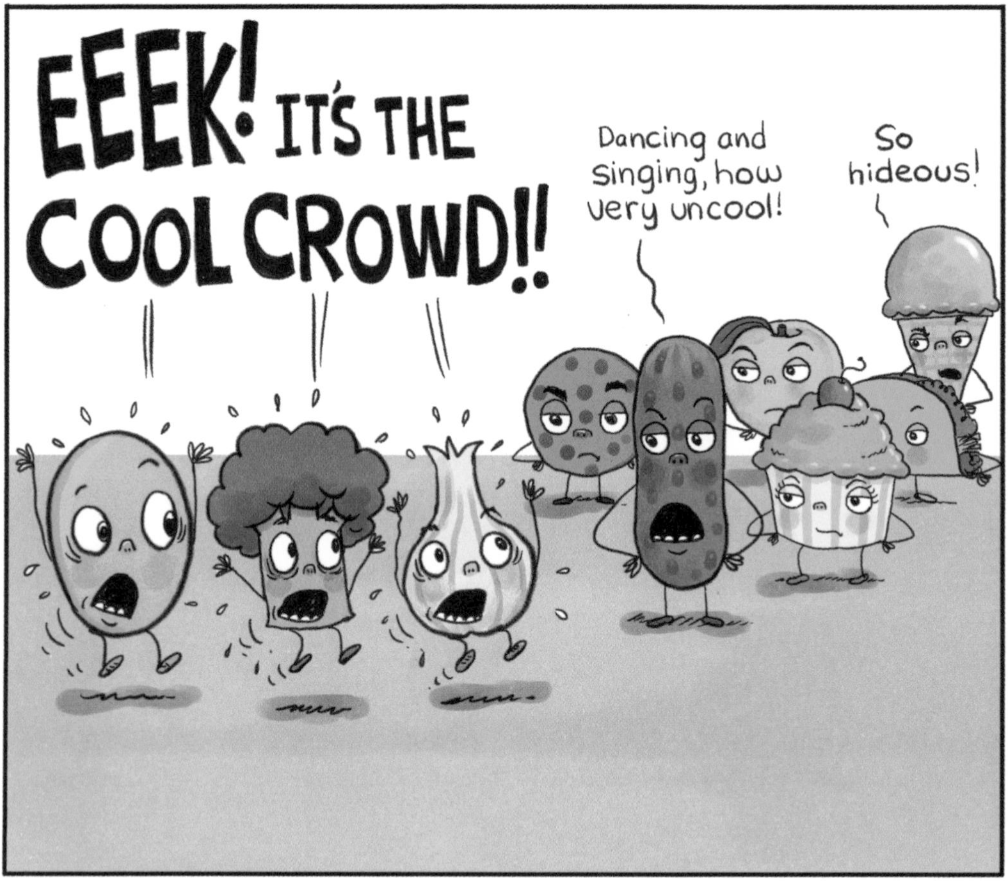
EEEK! IT'S THE COOL CROWD!!
Dancing and singing, how very uncool!
So hideous!

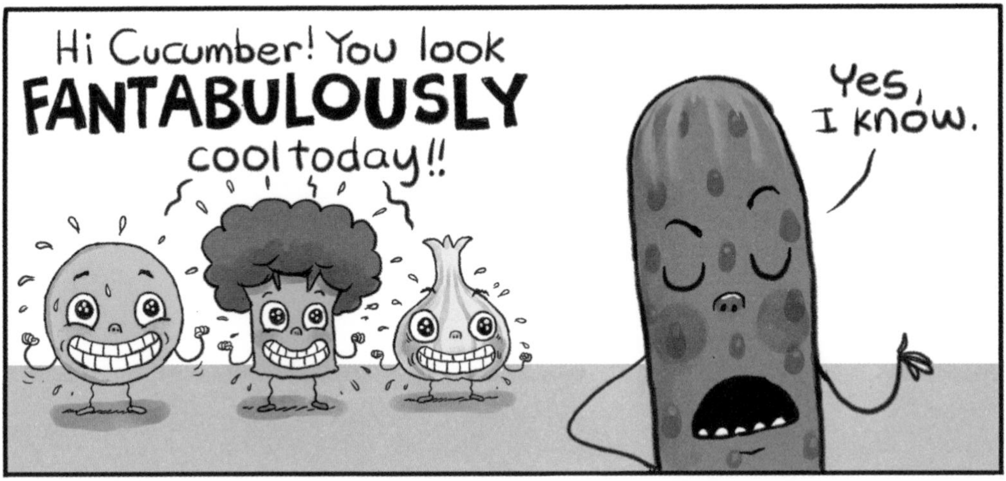
Hi Cucumber! You look **FANTABULOUSLY** cool today!!
Yes, I know.

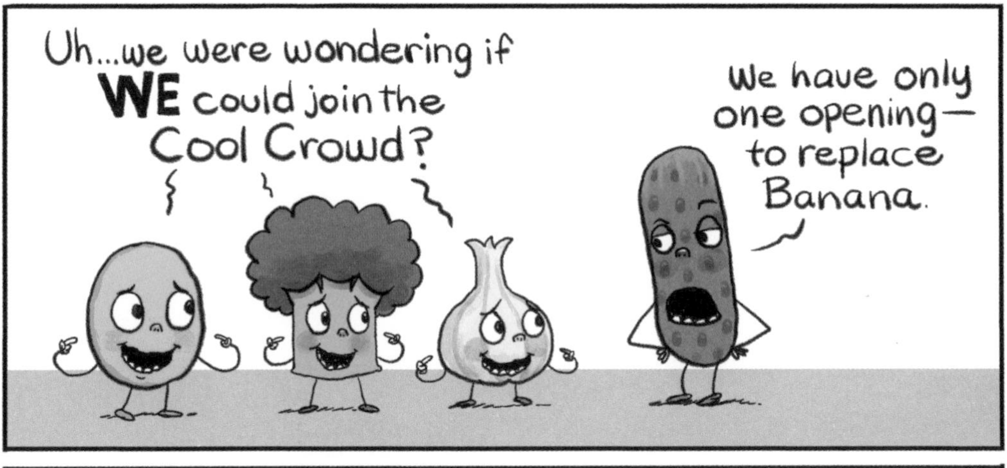
Uh...we were wondering if **WE** could join the Cool Crowd?
We have only one opening—to replace Banana.

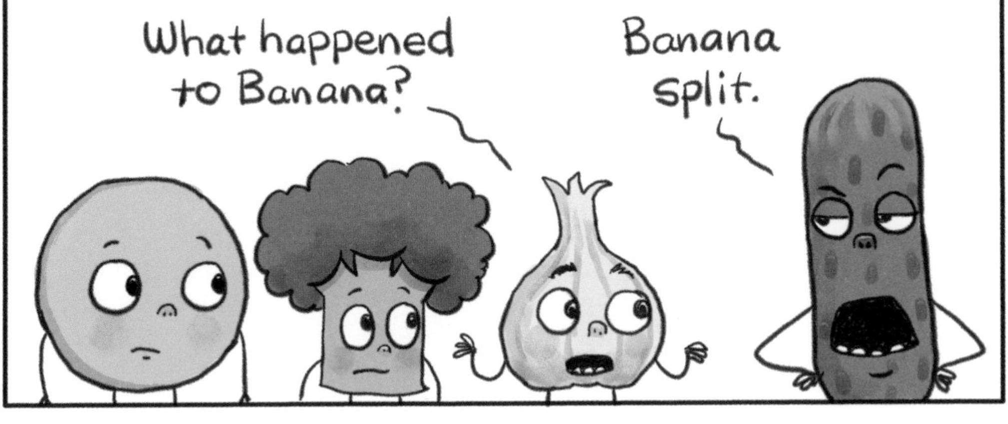
What happened to Banana?
Banana split.

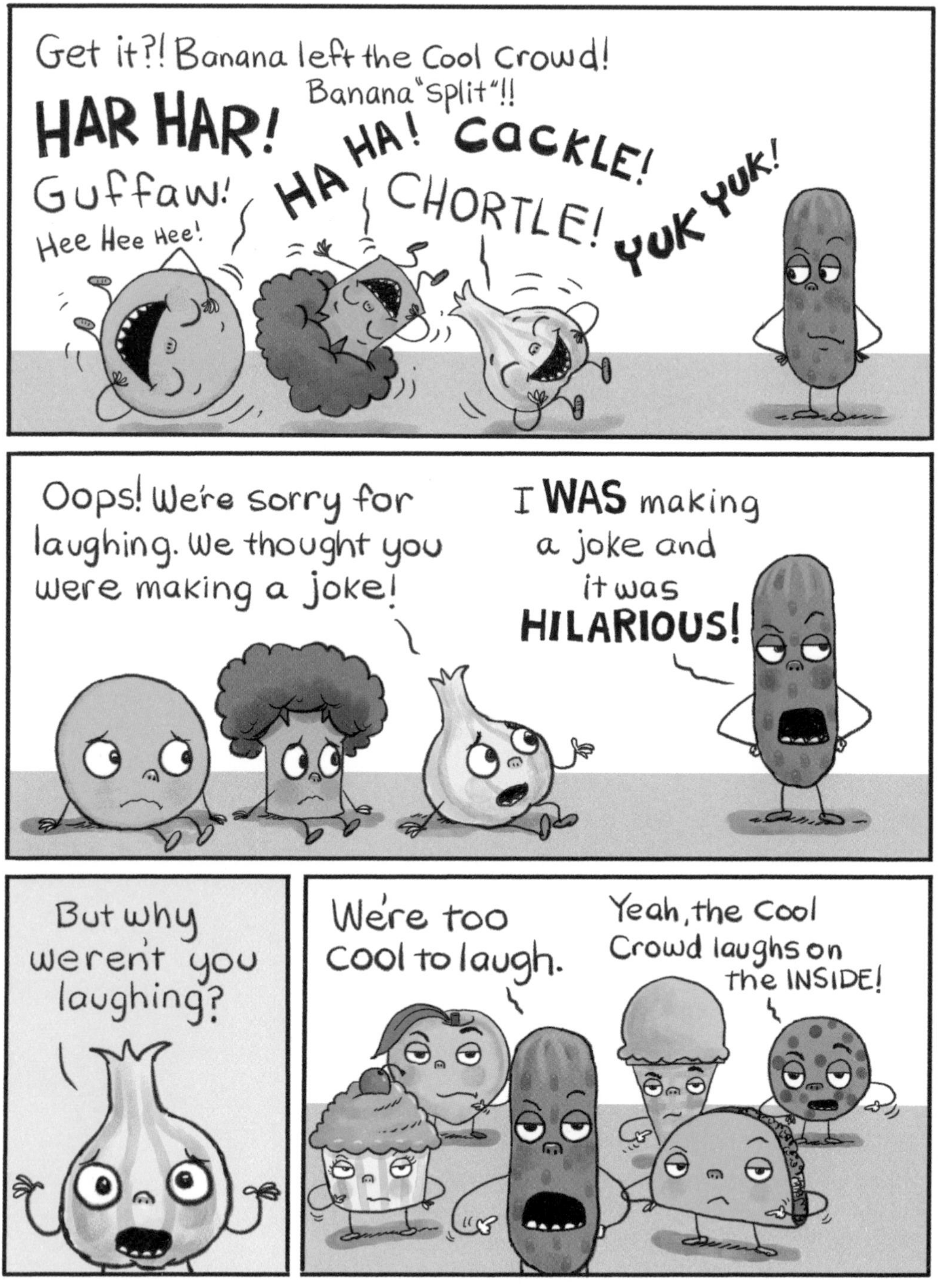

Get it?! Banana left the Cool Crowd!
Banana "split"!!
HAR HAR!
Guffaw!
Hee Hee Hee!
HA HA!
CACKLE!
CHORTLE!
YUK YUK!
Oops! We're sorry for laughing. We thought you were making a joke!
I WAS making a joke and it was HILARIOUS!
But why weren't you laughing?
We're too cool to laugh.
Yeah, the Cool Crowd laughs on the INSIDE!

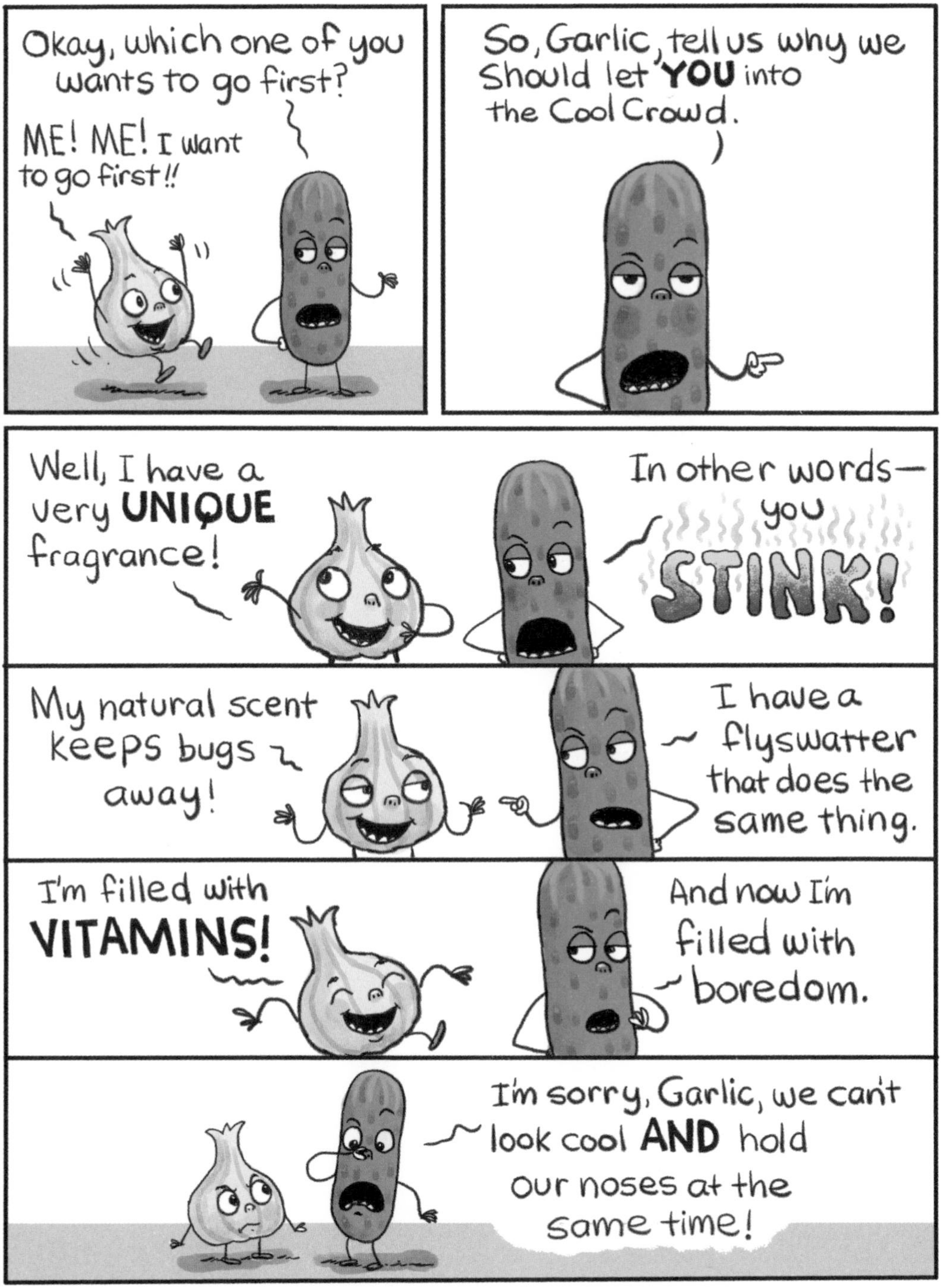

Okay, which one of you wants to go first?
ME! ME! I want to go first!!
So, Garlic, tell us why we should let YOU into the Cool Crowd.
Well, I have a very UNIQUE fragrance!
In other words— you STINK!
My natural scent keeps bugs away!
I have a flyswatter that does the same thing.
I'm filled with VITAMINS!
And now I'm filled with boredom.
I'm sorry, Garlic, we can't look cool AND hold our noses at the same time!

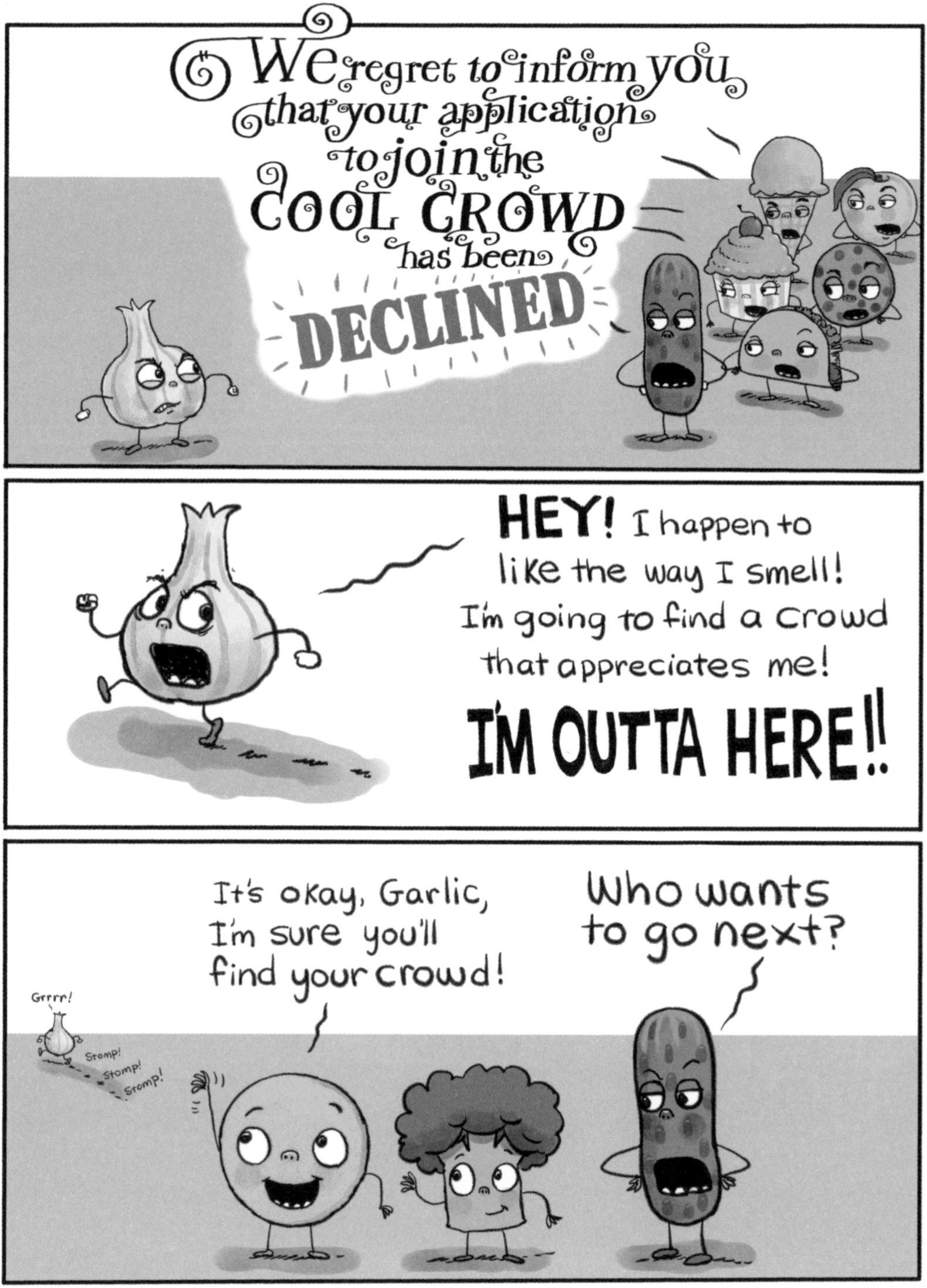
We regret to inform you that your application to join the COOL CROWD has been DECLINED
HEY! I happen to like the way I smell! I'm going to find a crowd that appreciates me!
I'M OUTTA HERE!!
Grrrr!
Stomp!
Stomp!
Stomp!
It's okay, Garlic, I'm sure you'll find your crowd!
Who wants to go next?

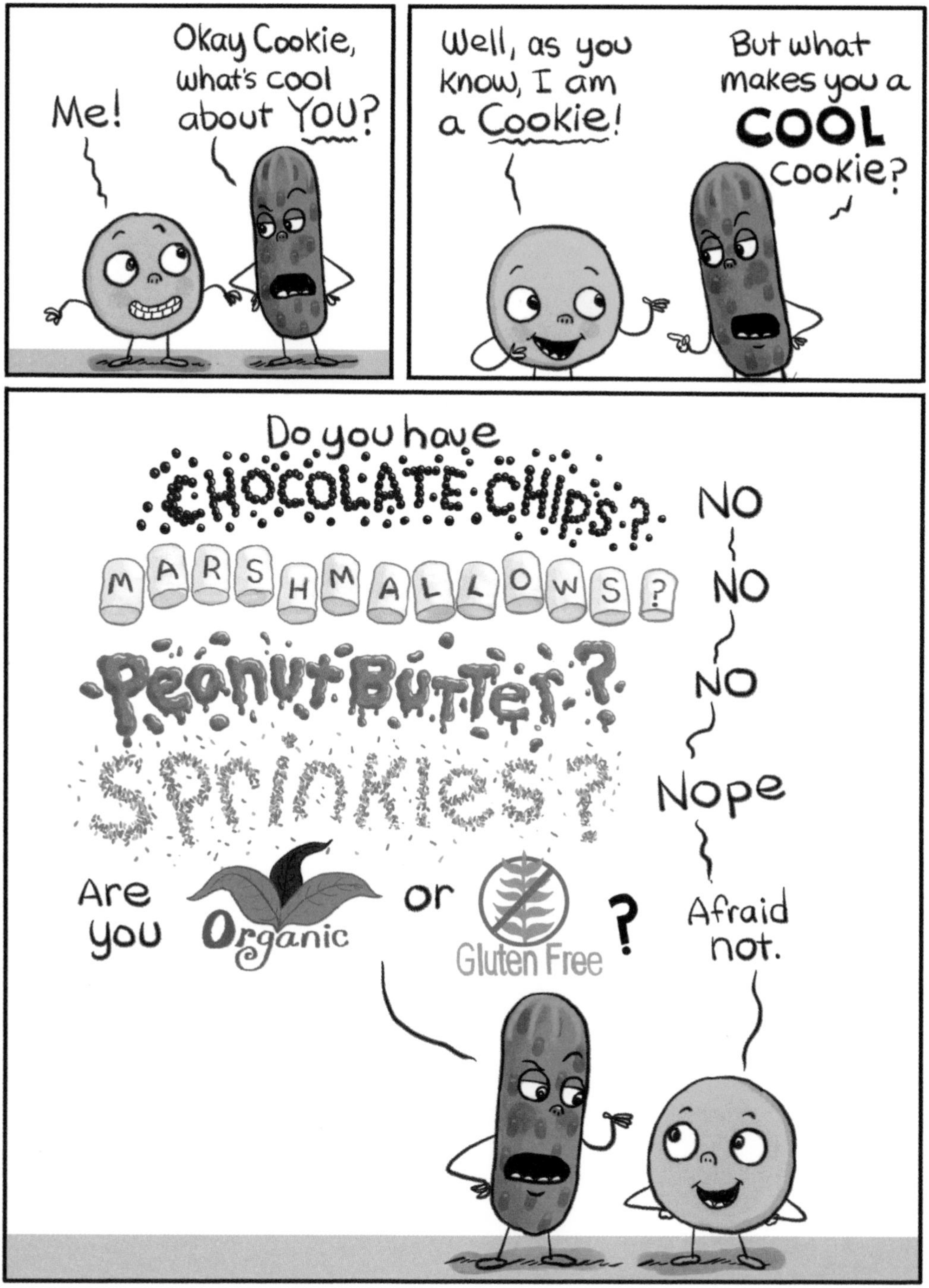
Okay Cookie, what's cool about YOU?
Me!
Well, as you know, I am a Cookie!
But what makes you a COOL cookie?
Do you have CHOCOLATE CHIPS?
NO
MARSHMALLOWS?
NO
Peanut Butter?
NO
Sprinkles?
Nope
Are you Organic or Gluten Free?
Afraid not.

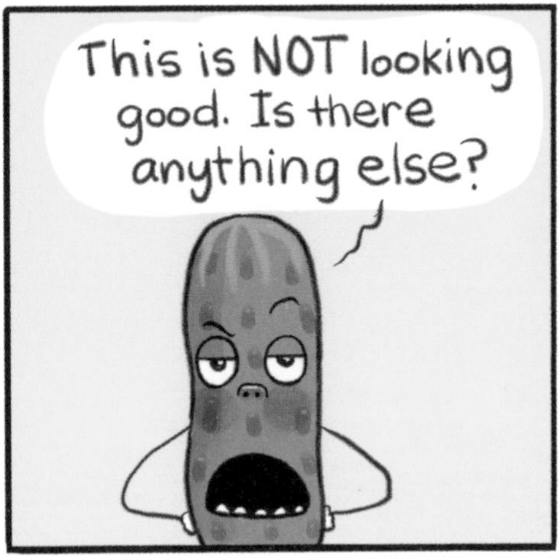
This is NOT looking good. Is there anything else?

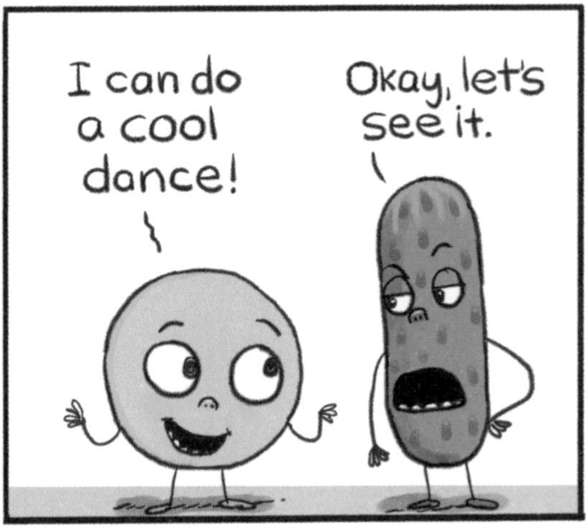
I can do a cool dance!
Okay, let's see it.

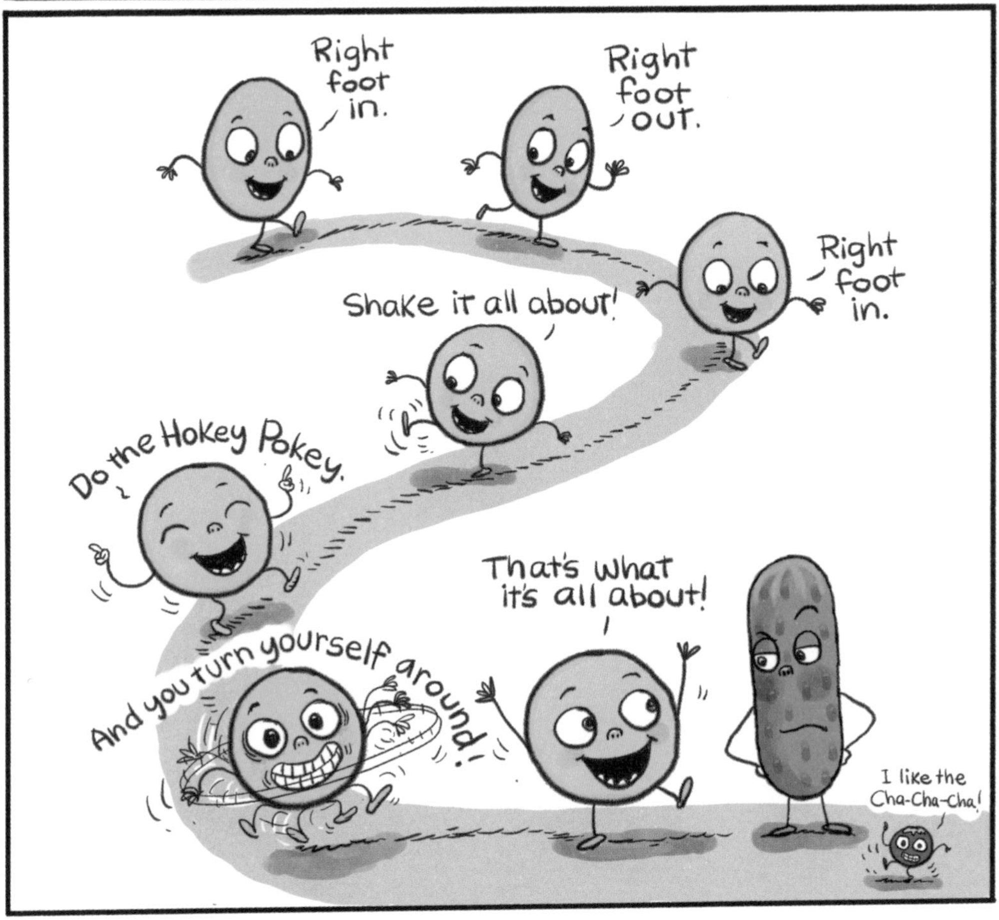
Right foot in.
Right foot out.
Right foot in.
Shake it all about!
Do the Hokey Pokey.
And you turn yourself around!
That's what it's all about!
I like the Cha-Cha-Cha!

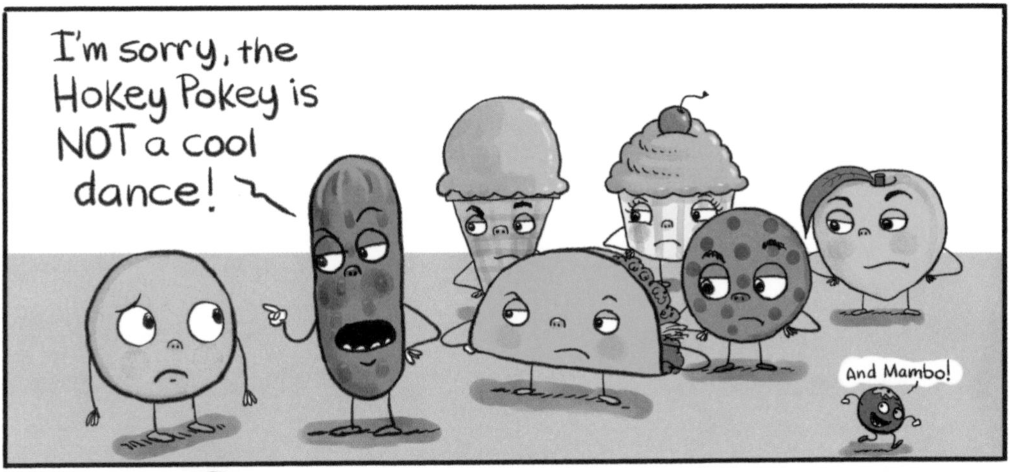
I'm sorry, the Hokey Pokey is NOT a cool dance!
And Mambo!

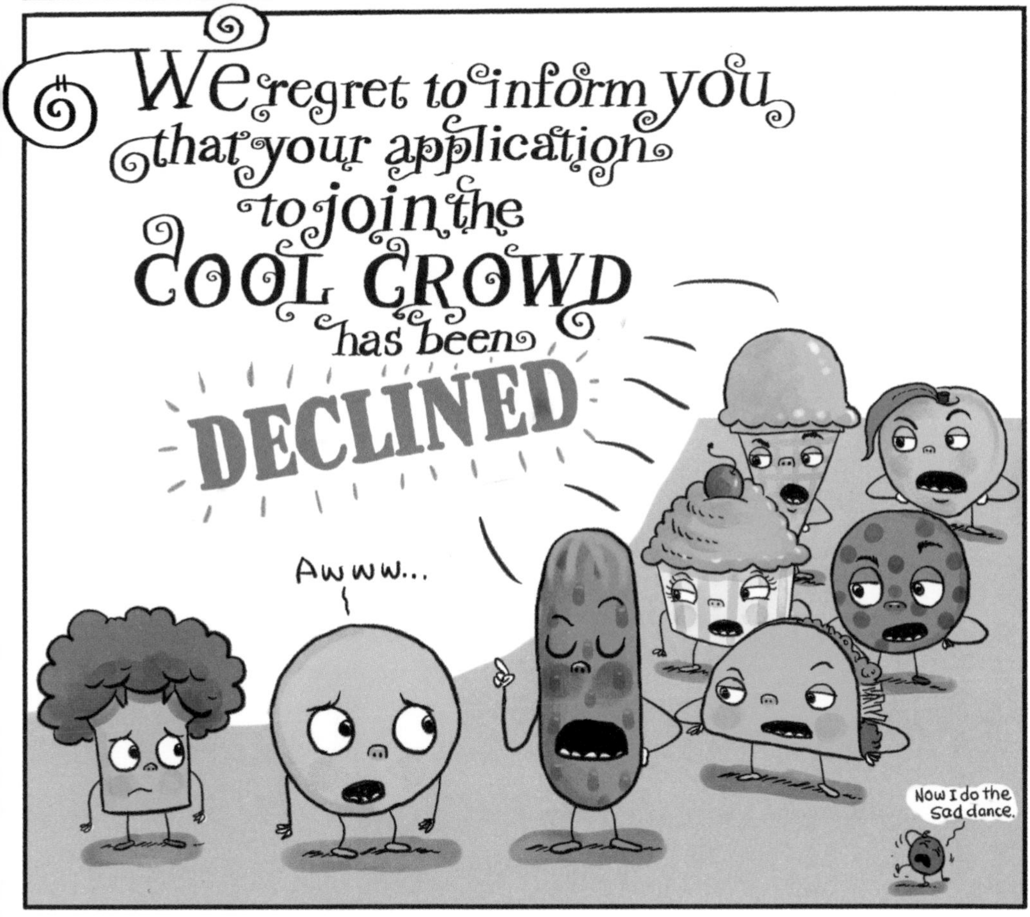
We regret to inform you that your application to join the COOL CROWD has been DECLINED
Awww...
Now I do the sad dance.

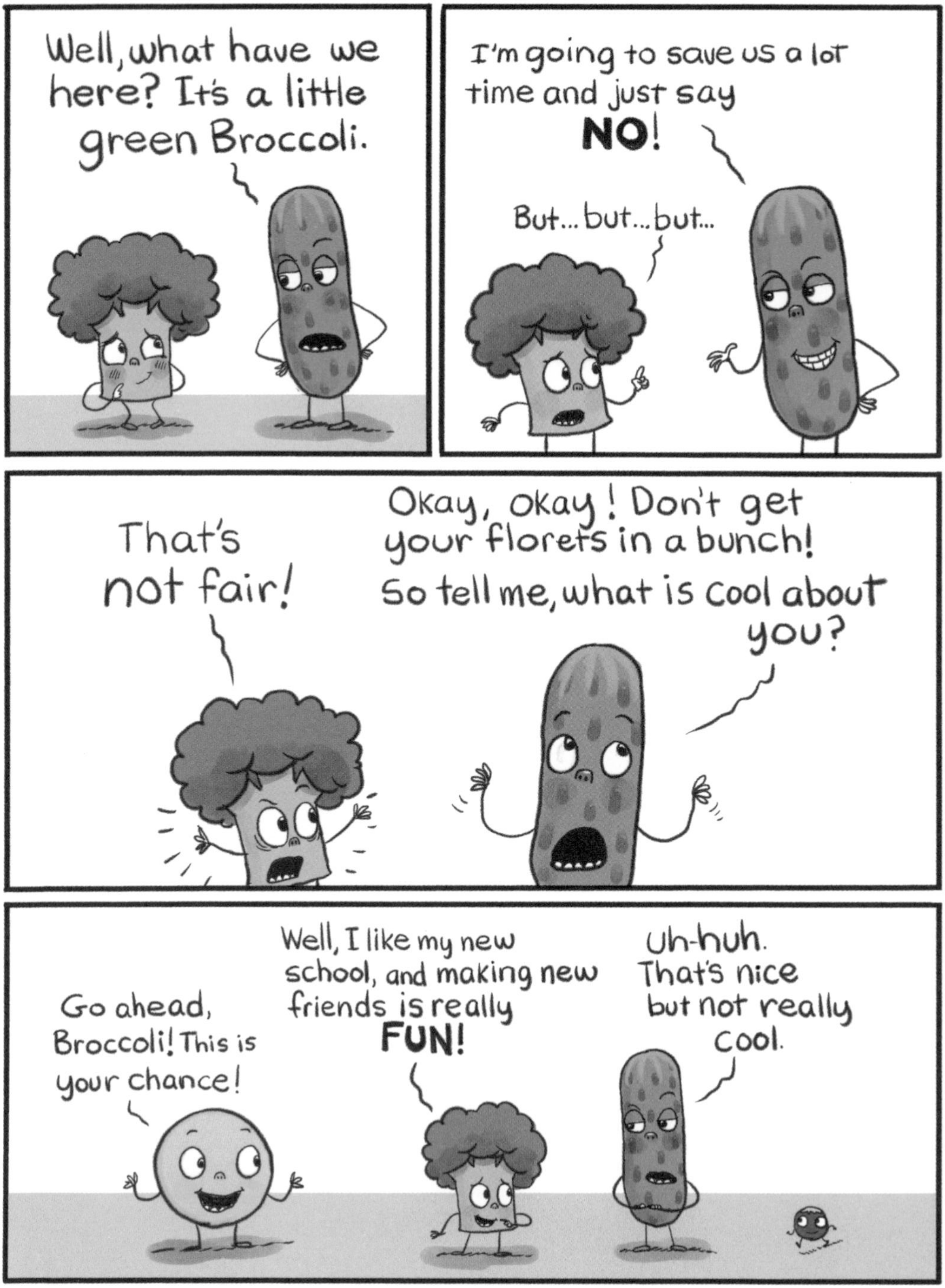

Well, what have we here? It's a little green Broccoli.
I'm going to save us a lot time and just say **NO**!
But... but... but...
That's not fair!
Okay, okay! Don't get your florets in a bunch! So tell me, what is cool about you?
Go ahead, Broccoli! This is your chance!
Well, I like my new school, and making new friends is really **FUN**!
Uh-huh. That's nice but not really cool.

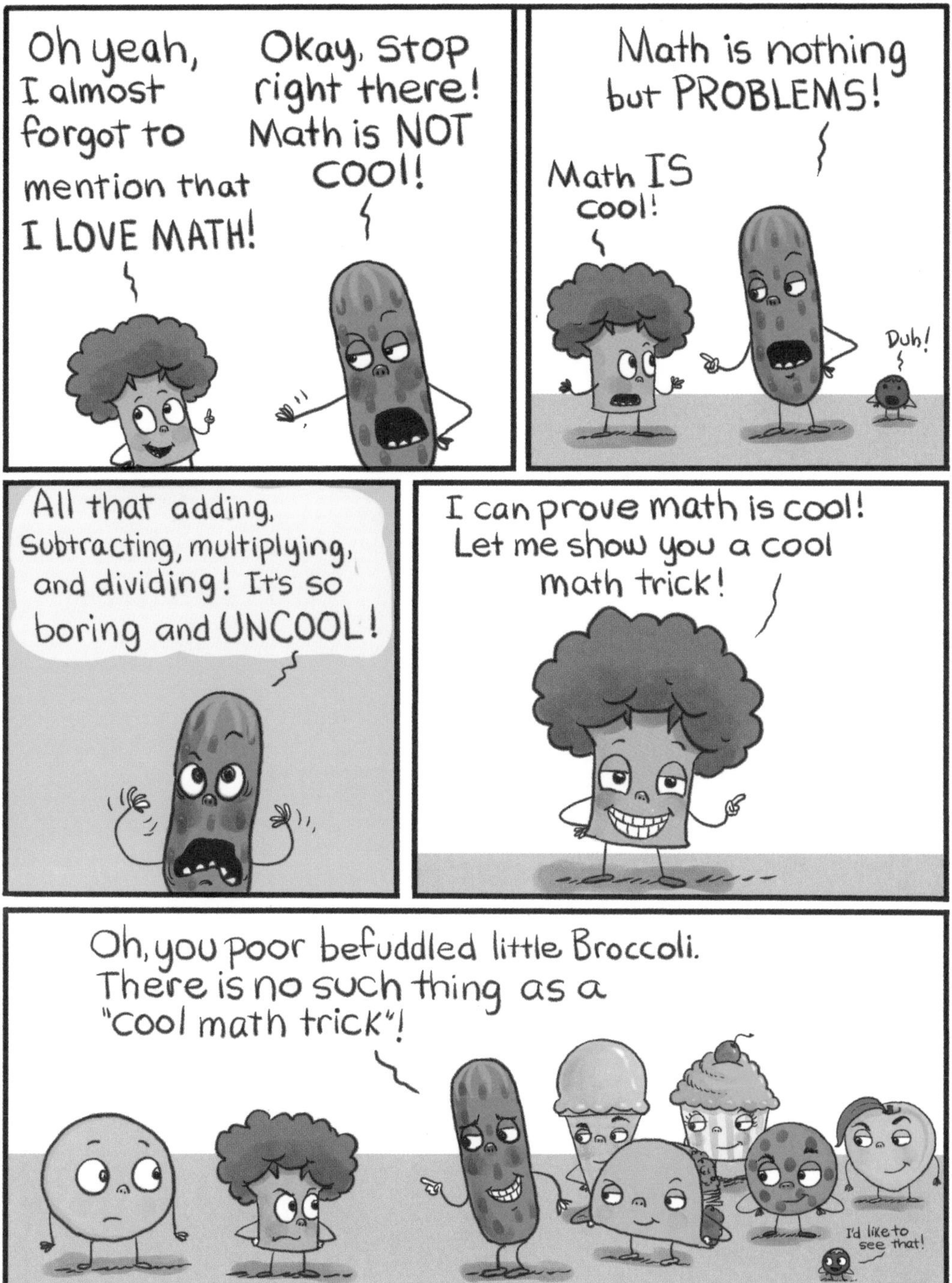
Oh yeah, I almost forgot to mention that I LOVE MATH!
Okay, Stop right there! Math is NOT COOl!
Math is nothing but PROBLEMS!
Math IS cool!
Duh!
All that adding, Subtracting, multiplying, and dividing! It's so boring and UNCOOL!
I can prove math is cool! Let me show you a cool math trick!
Oh, you poor befuddled little Broccoli. There is no such thing as a "cool math trick"!
I'd like to see that!

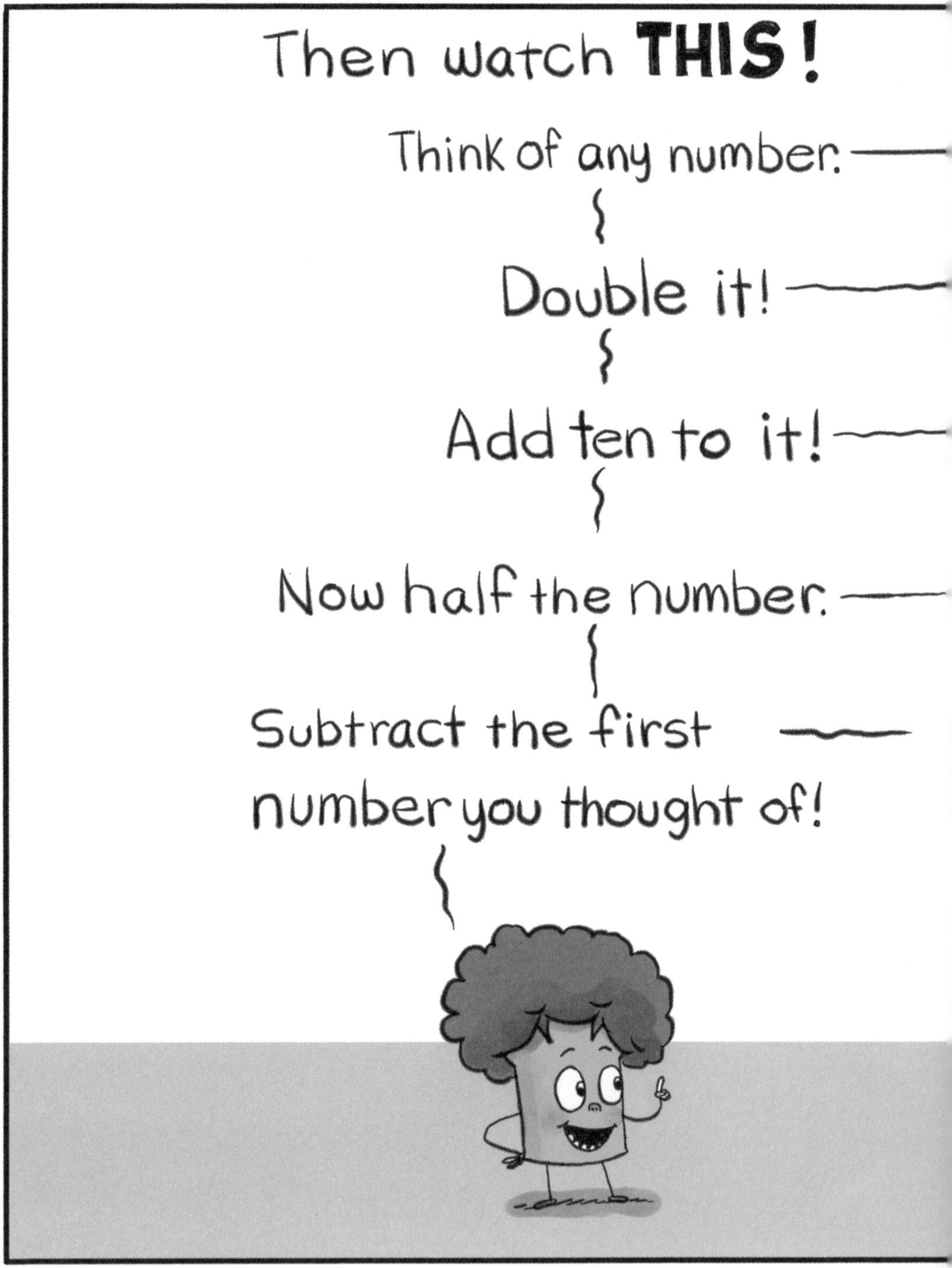
Then watch **THIS!**
Think of any number.
Double it!
Add ten to it!
Now half the number.
Subtract the first number you thought of!

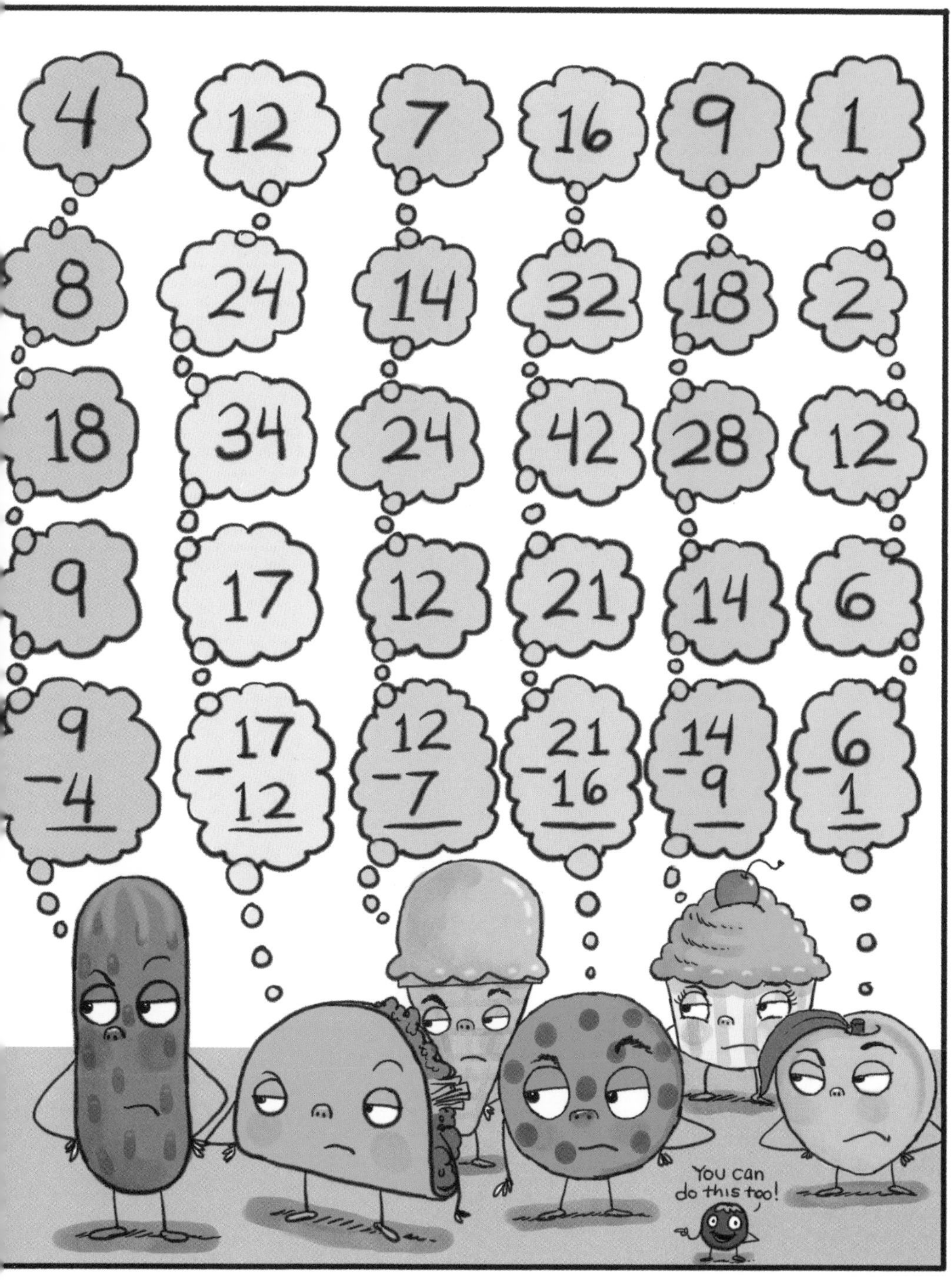
4 12 7 16 9 1
8 24 14 32 18 2
18 34 24 42 28 12
9 17 12 21 14 6
9 − 4
17 − 12
12 − 7
21 − 16
14 − 9
6 − 1
You can do this too!

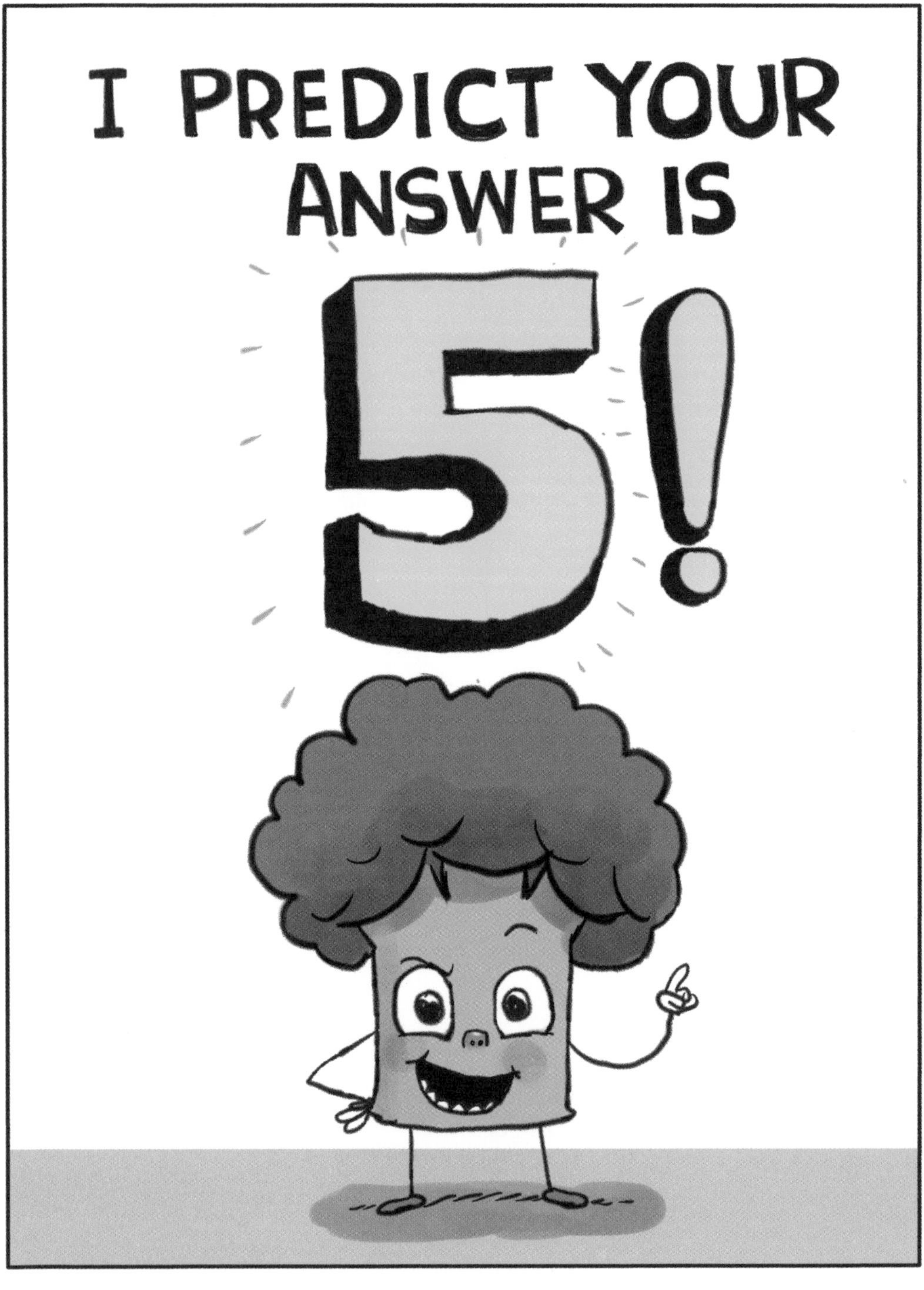
I PREDICT YOUR ANSWER IS
5!

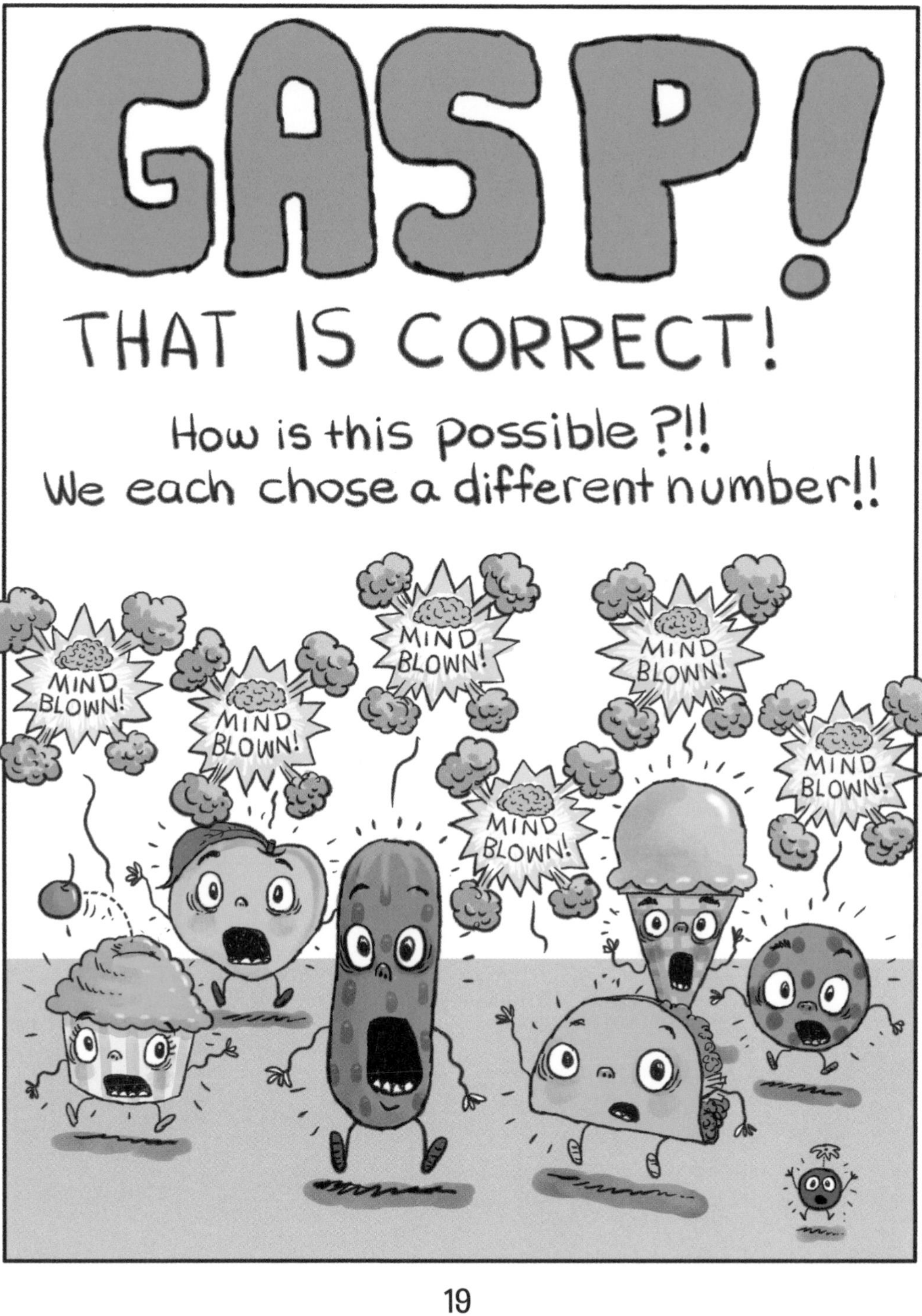
GASP!
THAT IS CORRECT!
How is this possible ?!!
We each chose a different number!!
MIND BLOWN!
MIND BLOWN!
MIND BLOWN!
MIND BLOWN!
MIND BLOWN!
MIND BLOWN!

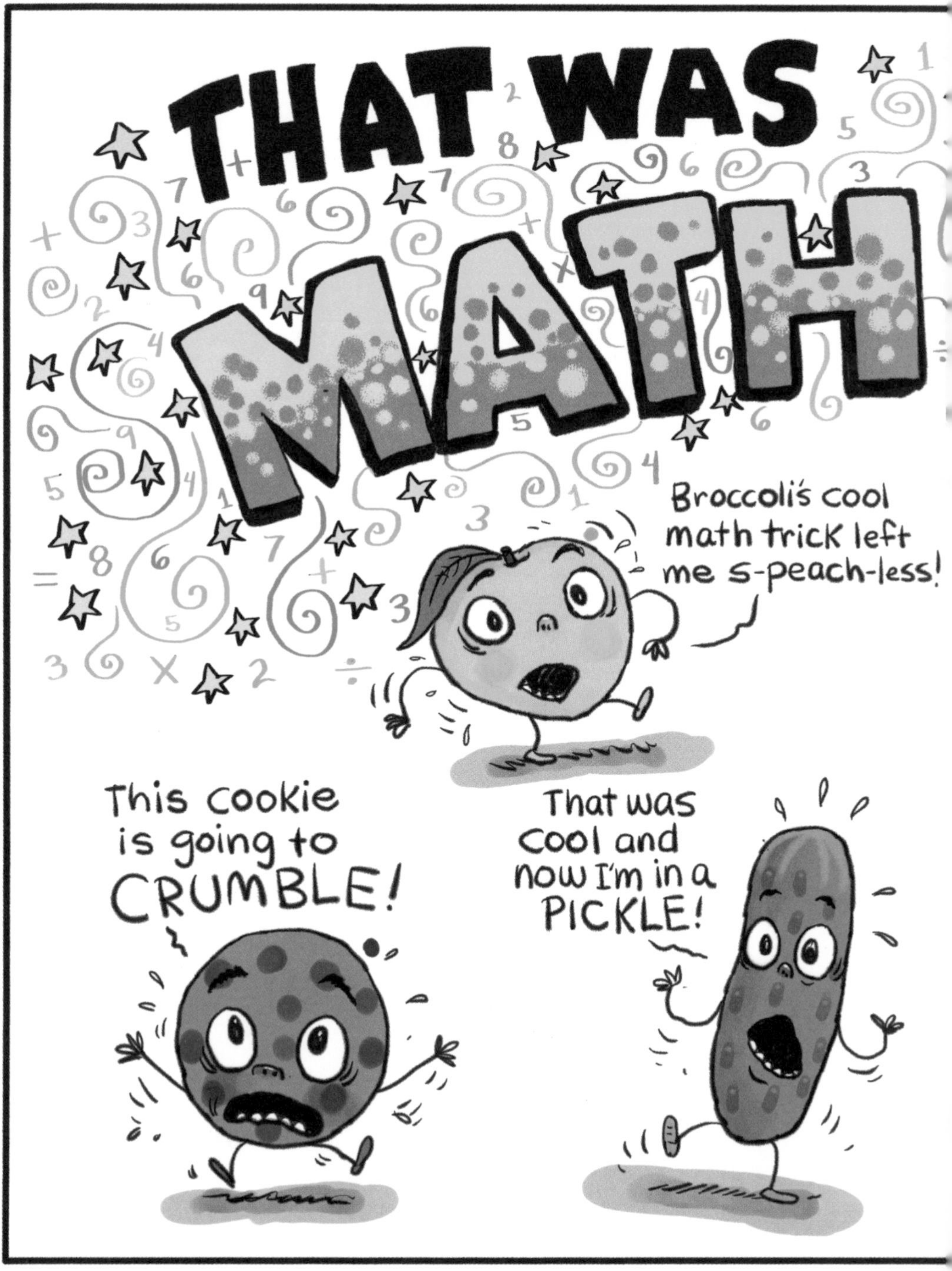
THAT WAS MATH
Broccoli's cool math trick left me s-peach-less!
This cookie is going to CRUMBLE!
That was cool and now I'm in a PICKLE!

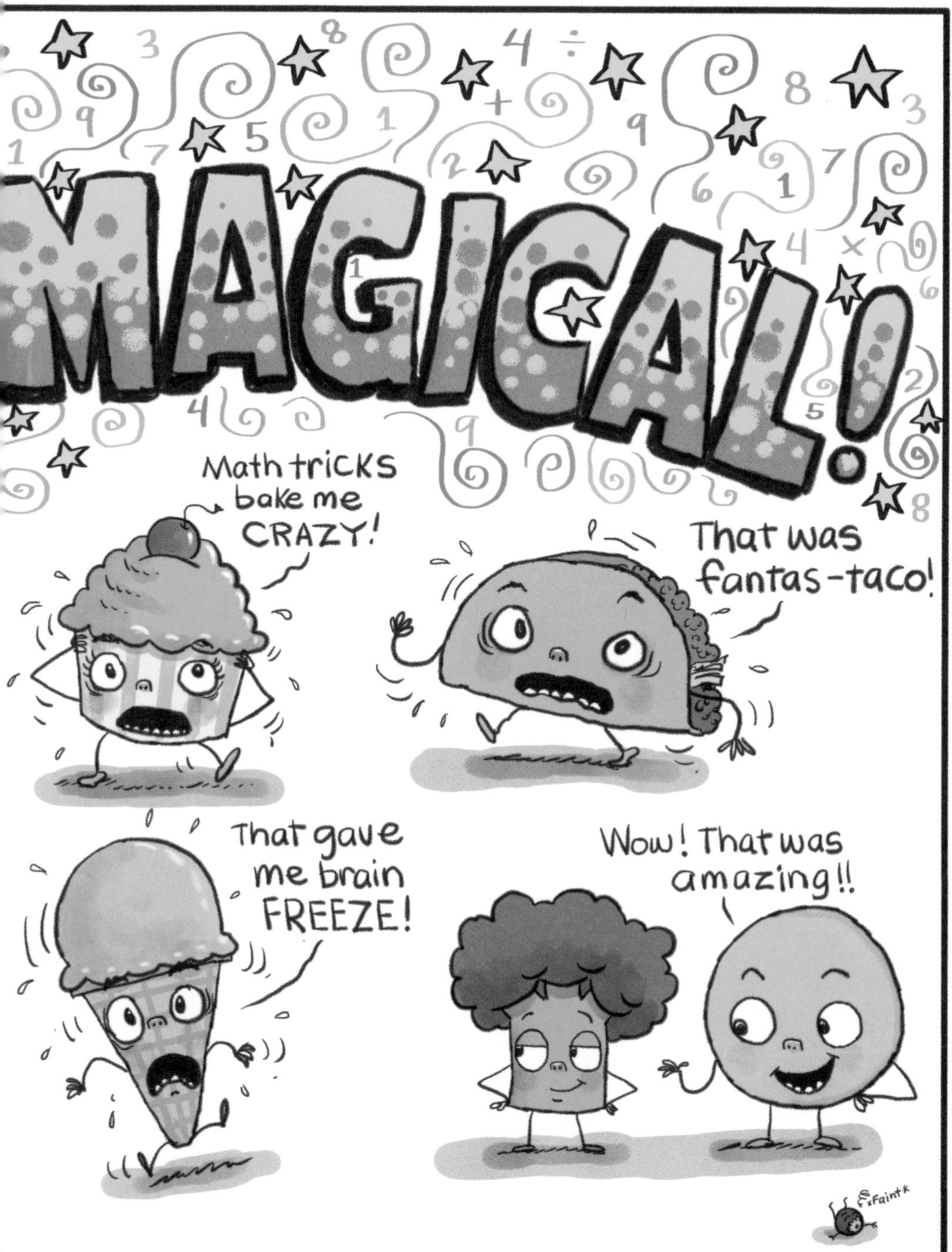
MAGICAL!
Math tricks bake me CRAZY!
That was fantas-taco!
That gave me brain FREEZE!
Wow! That was amazing!!

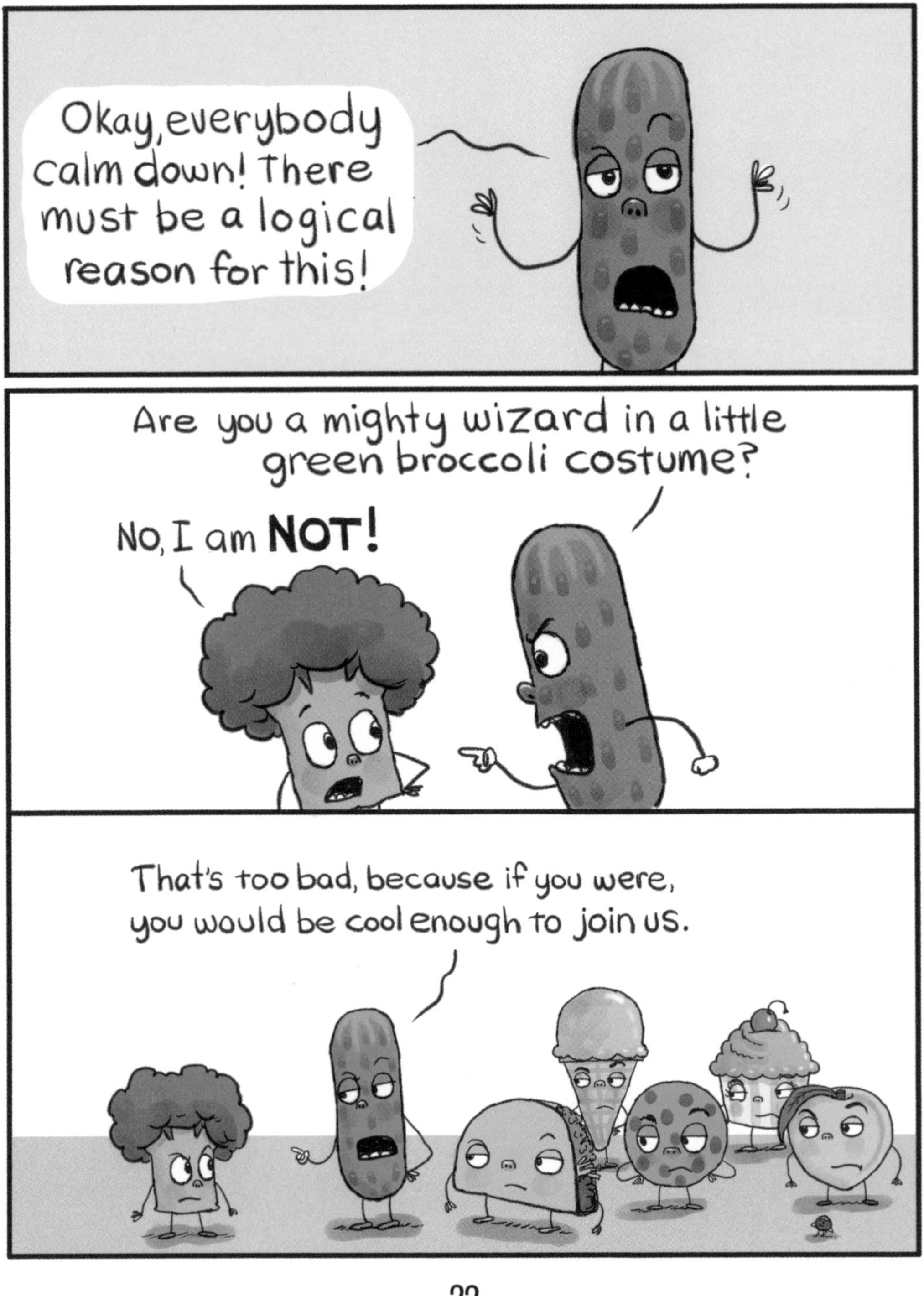
Okay, everybody calm down! There must be a logical reason for this!
Are you a mighty wizard in a little green broccoli costume?
No, I am **NOT**!
That's too bad, because if you were, you would be cool enough to join us.

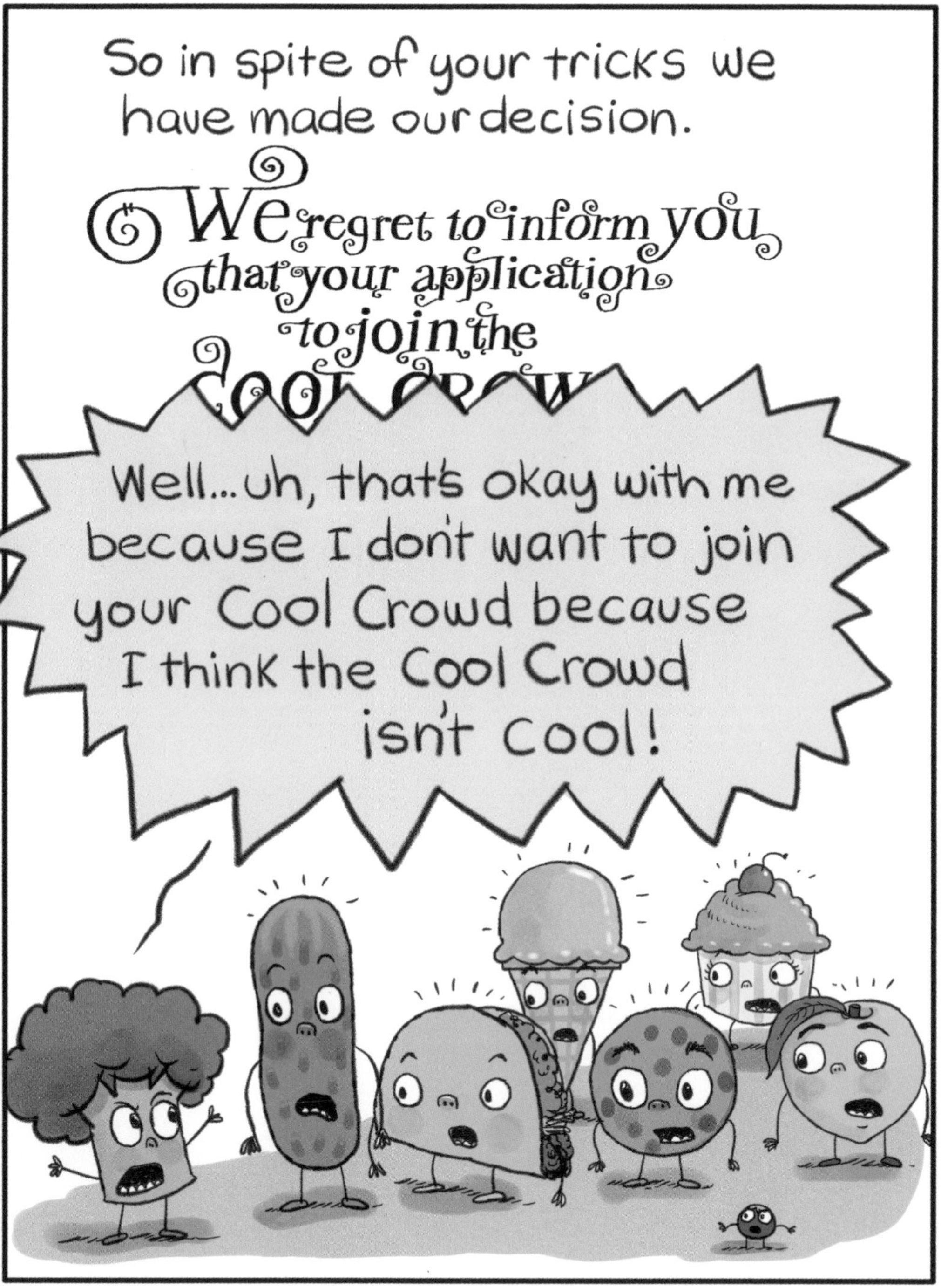
So in spite of your tricks we have made our decision.
We regret to inform you that your application to join the
Well...uh, that's okay with me because I don't want to join your Cool Crowd because I think the Cool Crowd isn't cool!

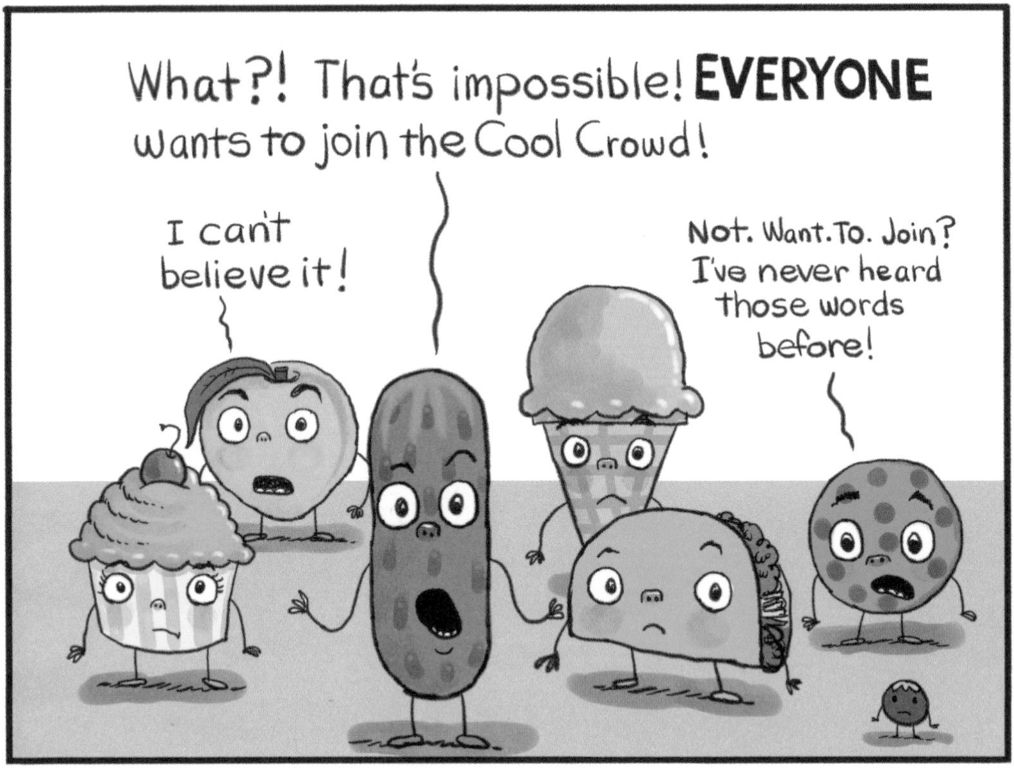
What?! That's impossible! **EVERYONE** wants to join the Cool Crowd!
I can't believe it!
Not. Want. To. Join? I've never heard those words before!

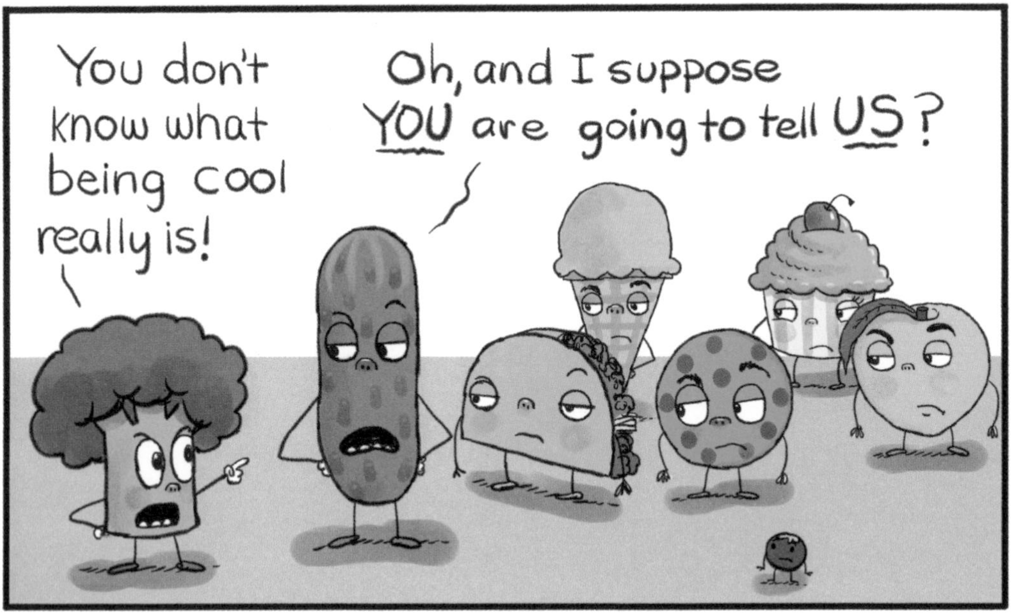
You don't know what being cool really is!
Oh, and I suppose YOU are going to tell US?

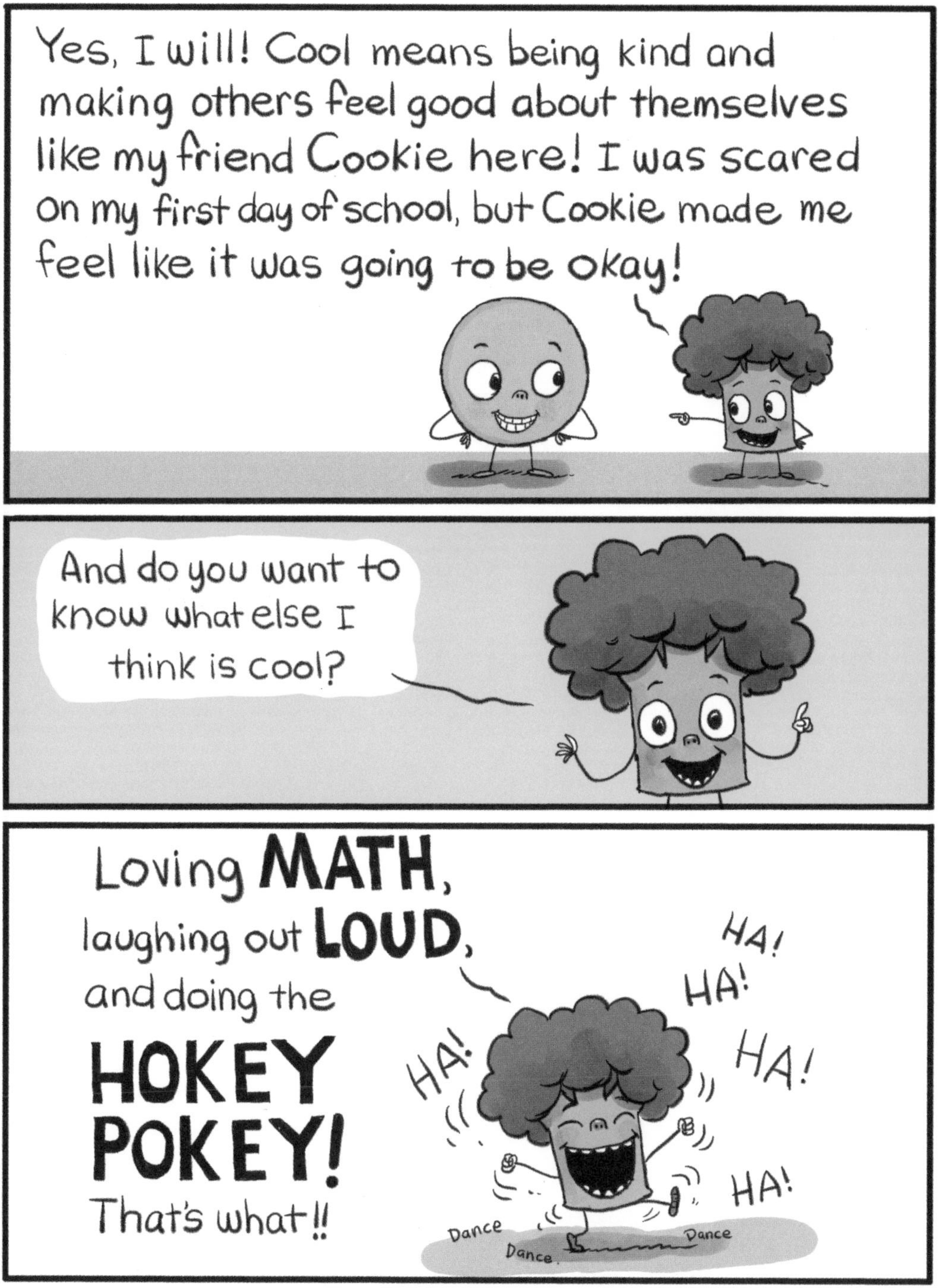
Yes, I will! Cool means being kind and making others feel good about themselves like my friend Cookie here! I was scared on my first day of school, but Cookie made me feel like it was going to be okay!
And do you want to know what else I think is cool?
Loving MATH, laughing out LOUD, and doing the HOKEY POKEY! That's what!!
HA!
HA!
HA!
HA!
HA!
Dance
Dance
Dance

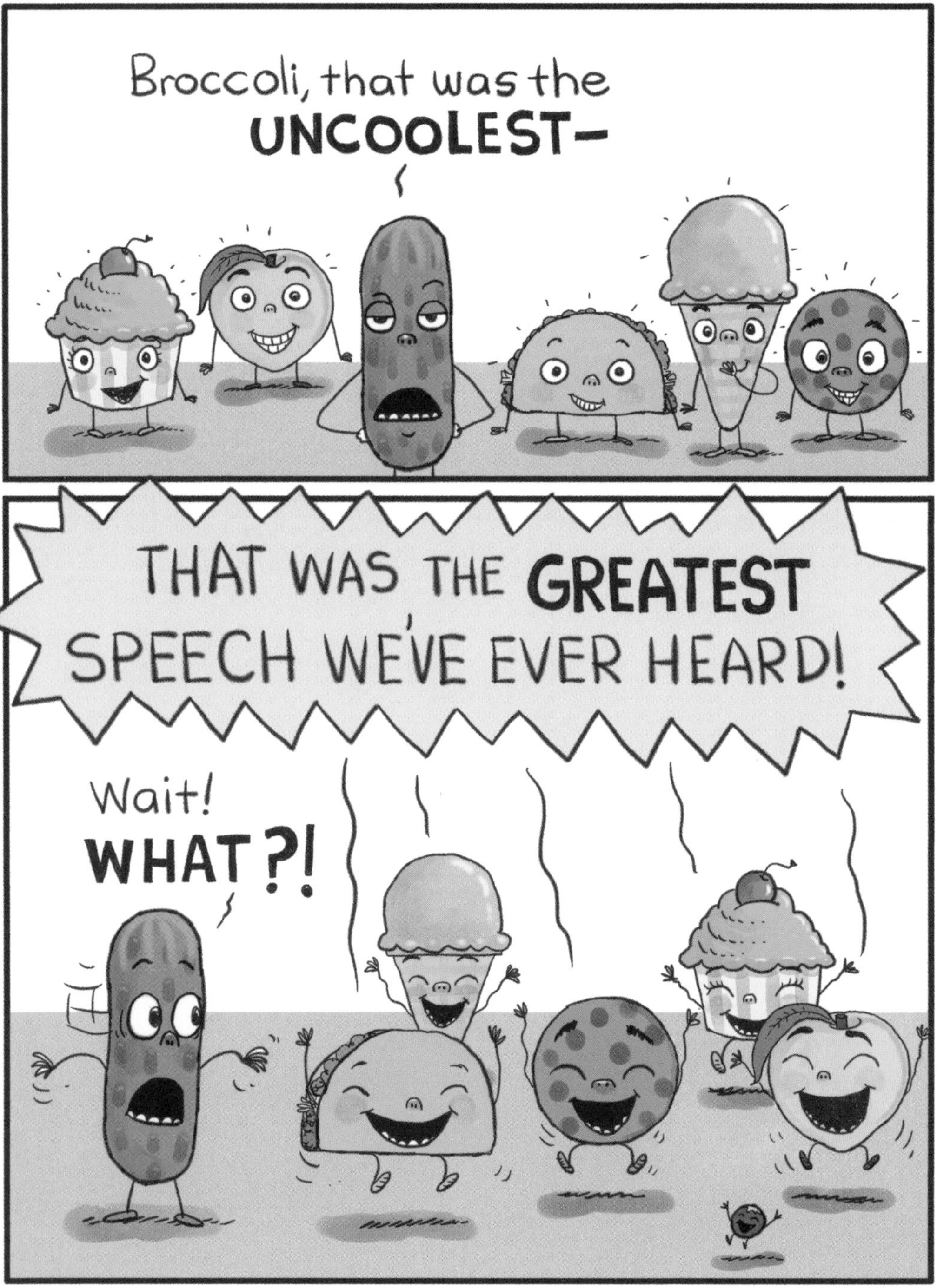
Broccoli, that was the UNCOOLEST–
THAT WAS THE GREATEST SPEECH WE'VE EVER HEARD!
Wait! WHAT?!

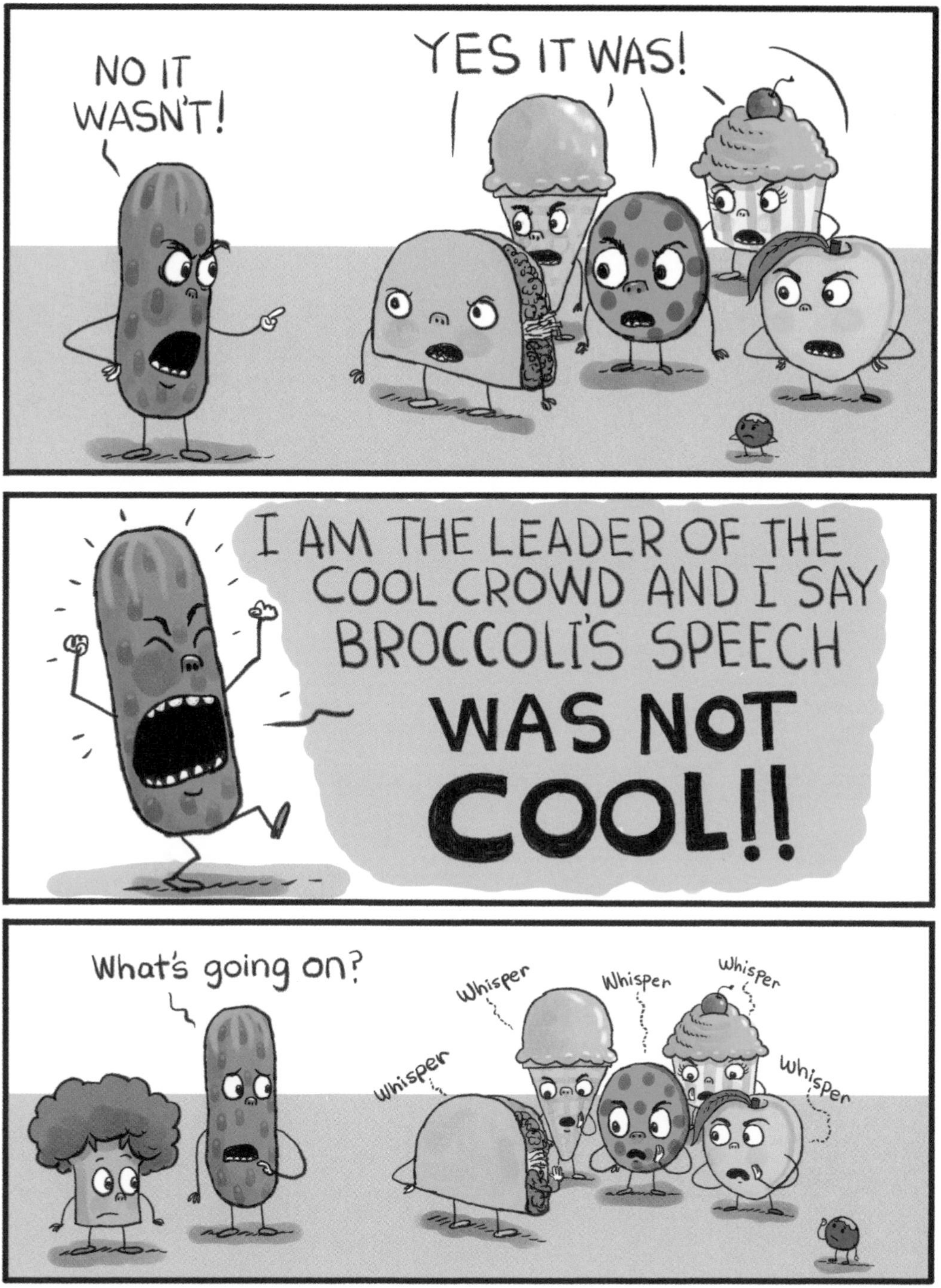
NO IT WASN'T!
YES IT WAS!
I AM THE LEADER OF THE COOL CROWD AND I SAY BROCCOLI'S SPEECH **WAS NOT COOL!!**
What's going on?
Whisper
Whisper
Whisper
Whisper
Whisper

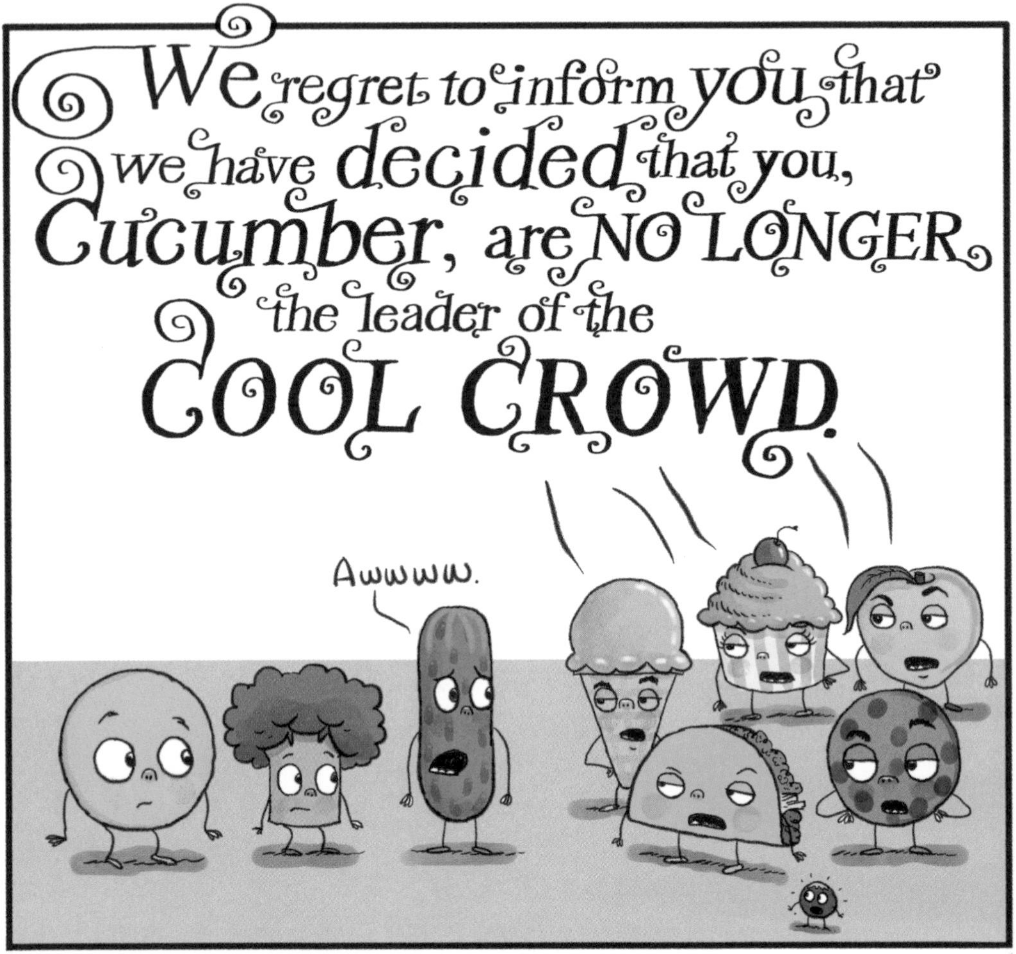
We regret to inform you that we have decided that you, Cucumber, are NO LONGER the leader of the COOL CROWD.
Awwww.
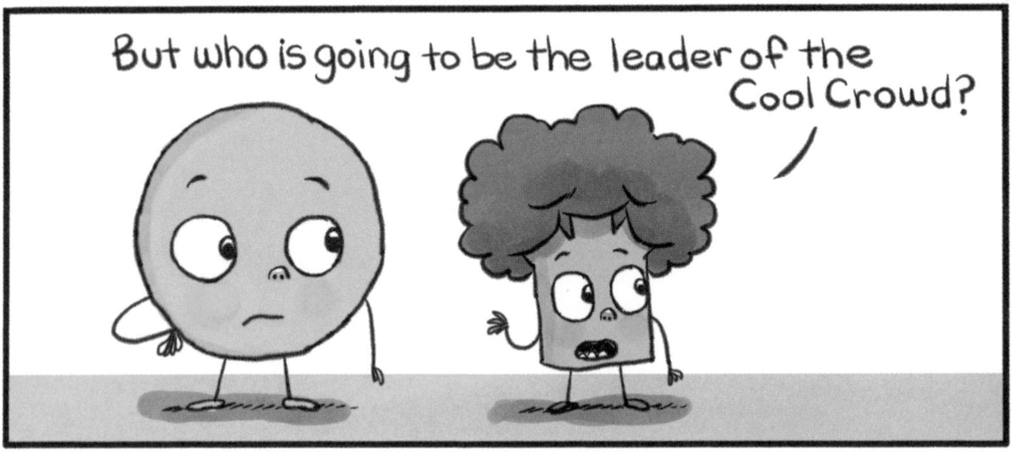
But who is going to be the leader of the Cool Crowd?

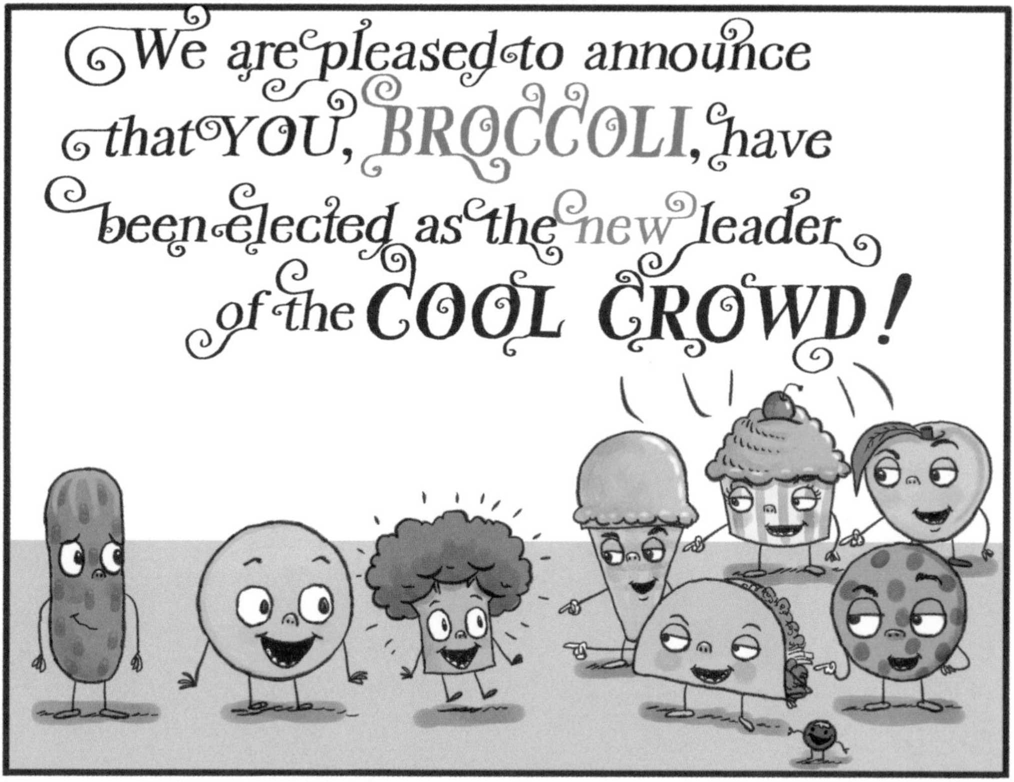
We are pleased to announce that YOU, BROCCOLI, have been elected as the new leader of the COOL CROWD!

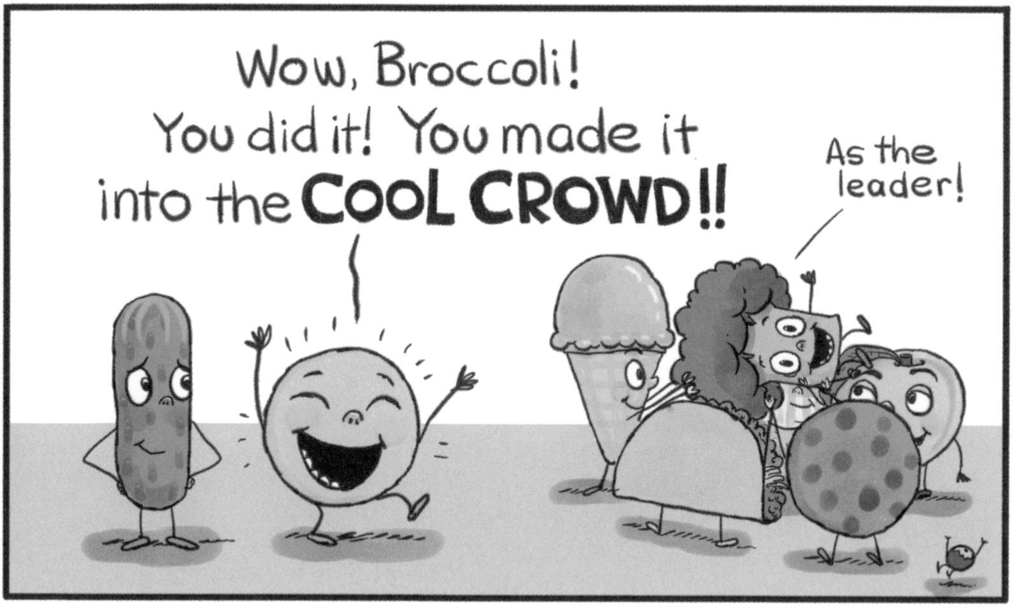
Wow, Broccoli! You did it! You made it into the COOL CROWD!!
As the leader!

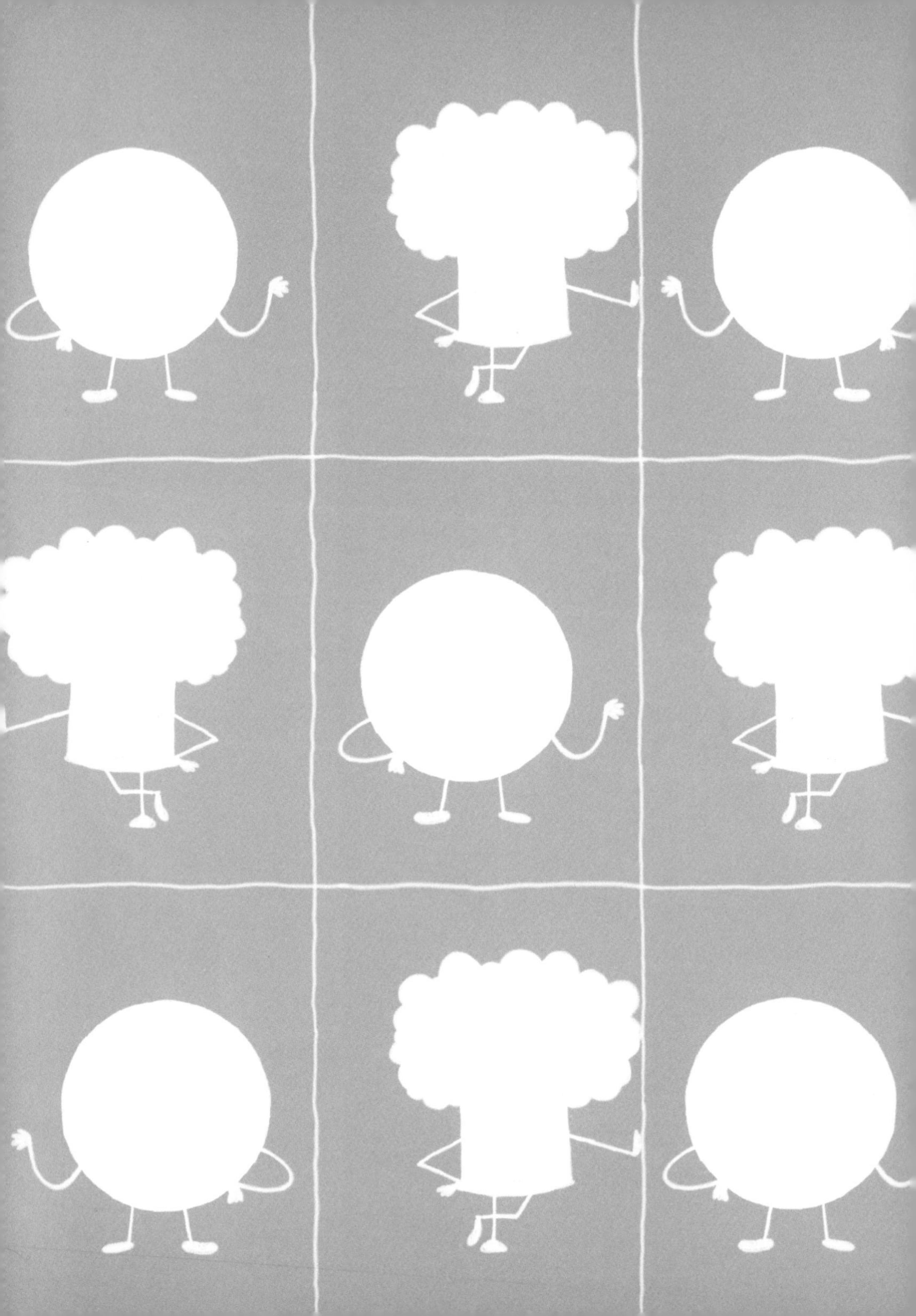

Chapter 2

BROCCOLI
DECIDES
WHAT IS COOL
AND
WHAT IS NOT!

Go ahead and ask me!

Broccoli is so Cooool!

Cool face

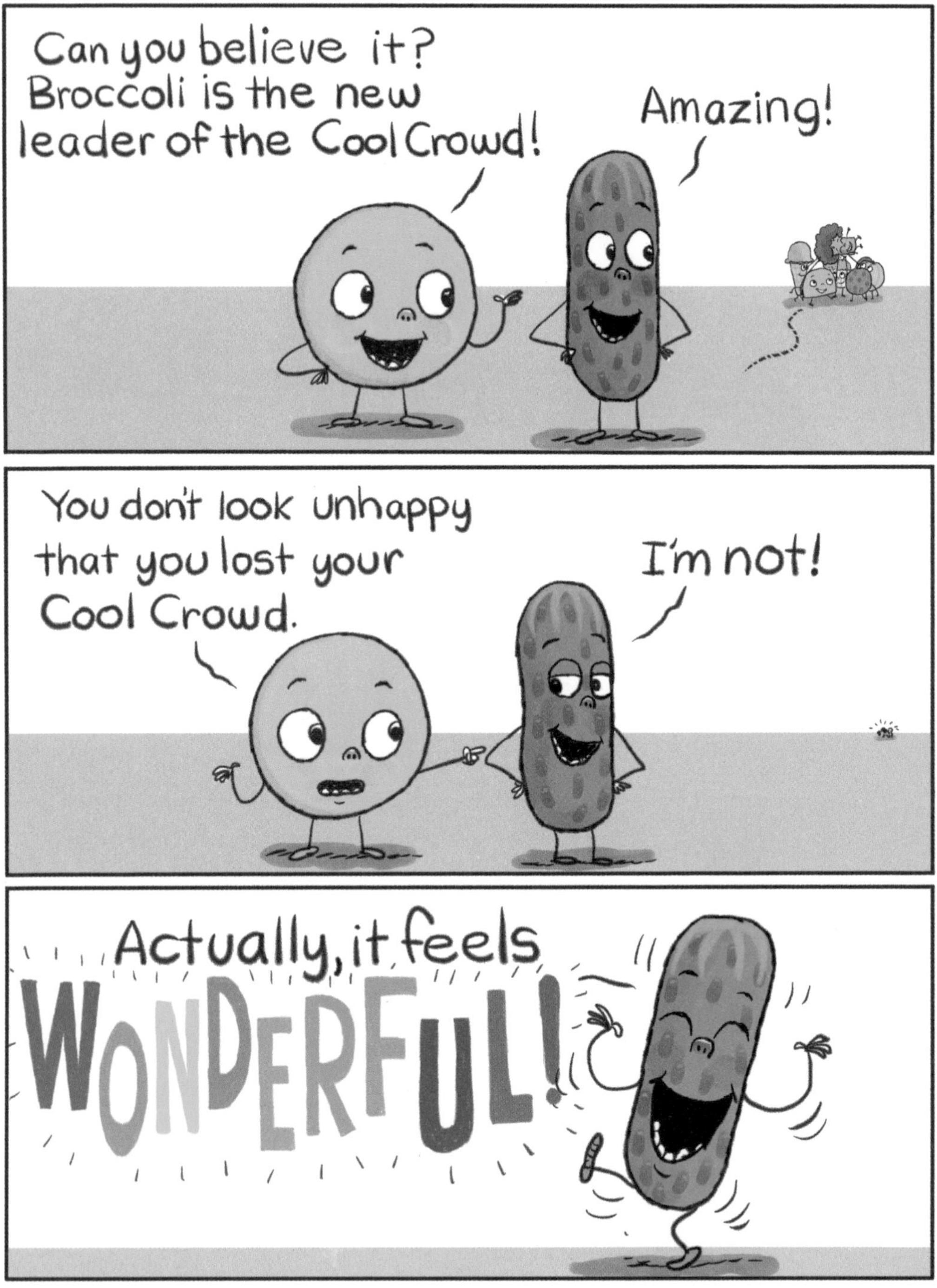
Can you believe it? Broccoli is the new leader of the Cool Crowd!
Amazing!
You don't look unhappy that you lost your Cool Crowd.
I'm not!
Actually, it feels
WONDERFUL!

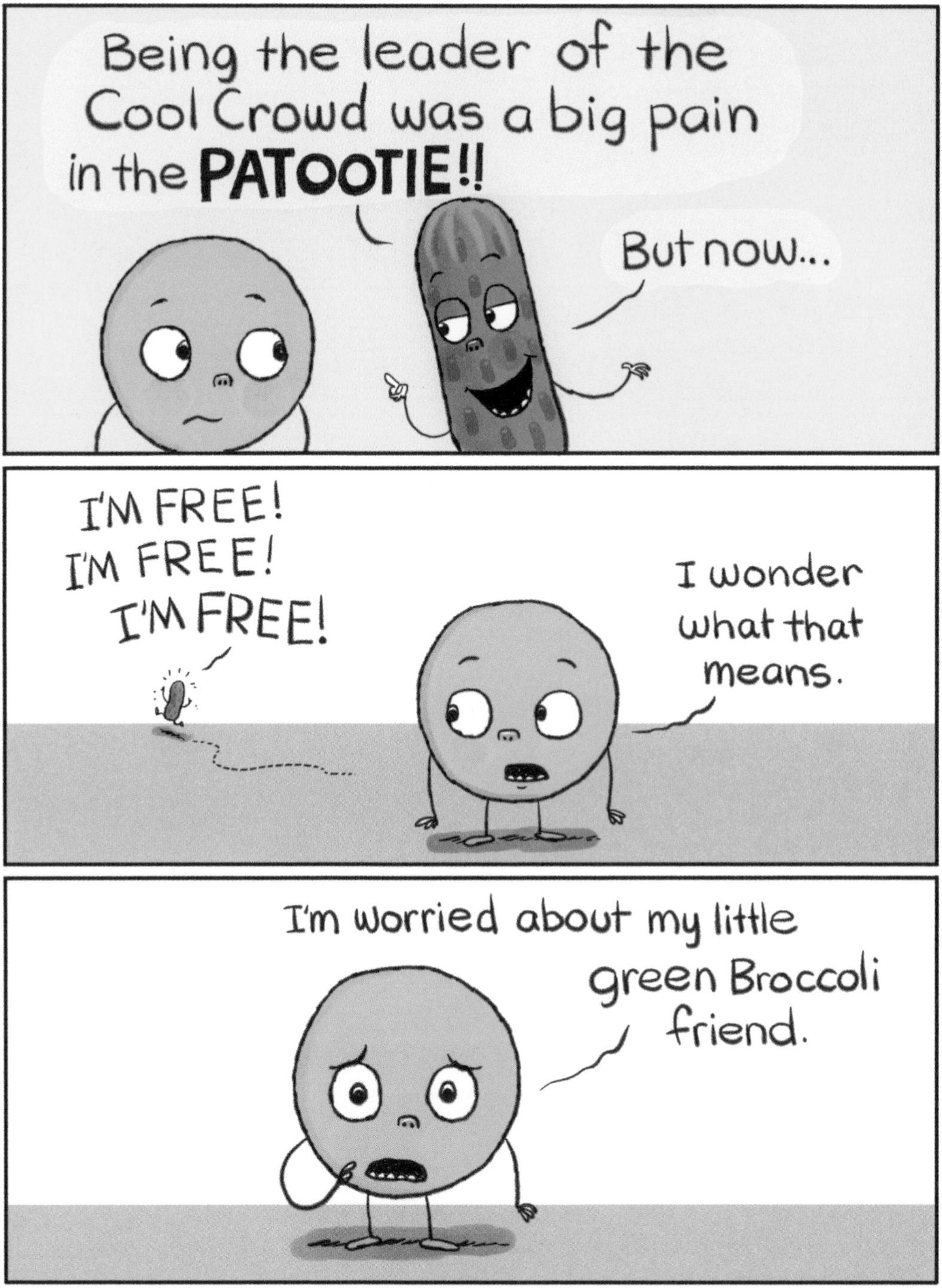

Being the leader of the Cool Crowd was a big pain in the PATOOTIE!!
But now...
I'M FREE! I'M FREE! I'M FREE!
I wonder what that means.
I'm worried about my little green Broccoli friend.

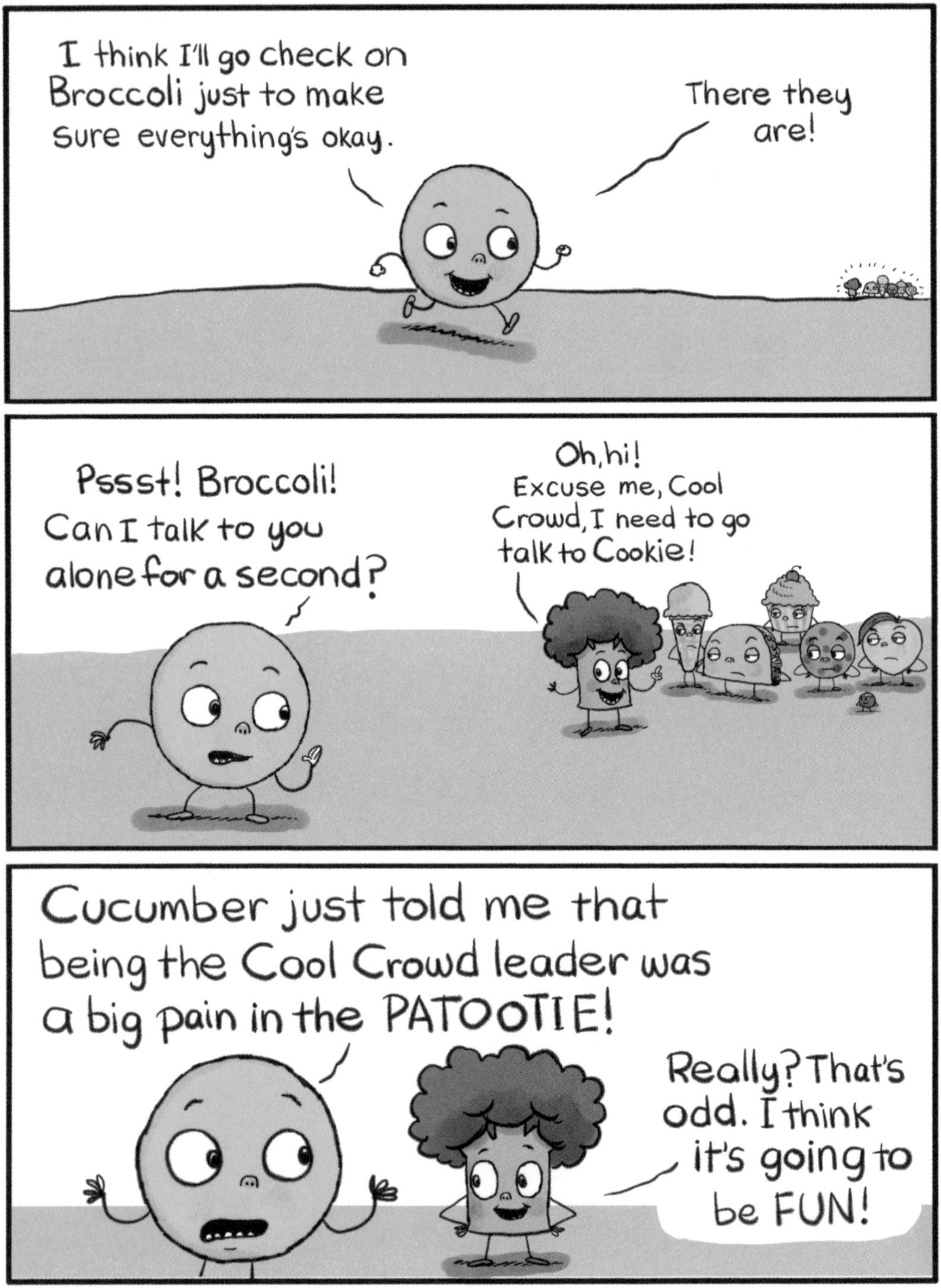
I think I'll go check on Broccoli just to make sure everything's okay.
There they are!
Pssst! Broccoli! Can I talk to you alone for a second?
Oh, hi! Excuse me, Cool Crowd, I need to go talk to Cookie!
Cucumber just told me that being the Cool Crowd leader was a big pain in the PATOOTIE!
Really? That's odd. I think it's going to be FUN!

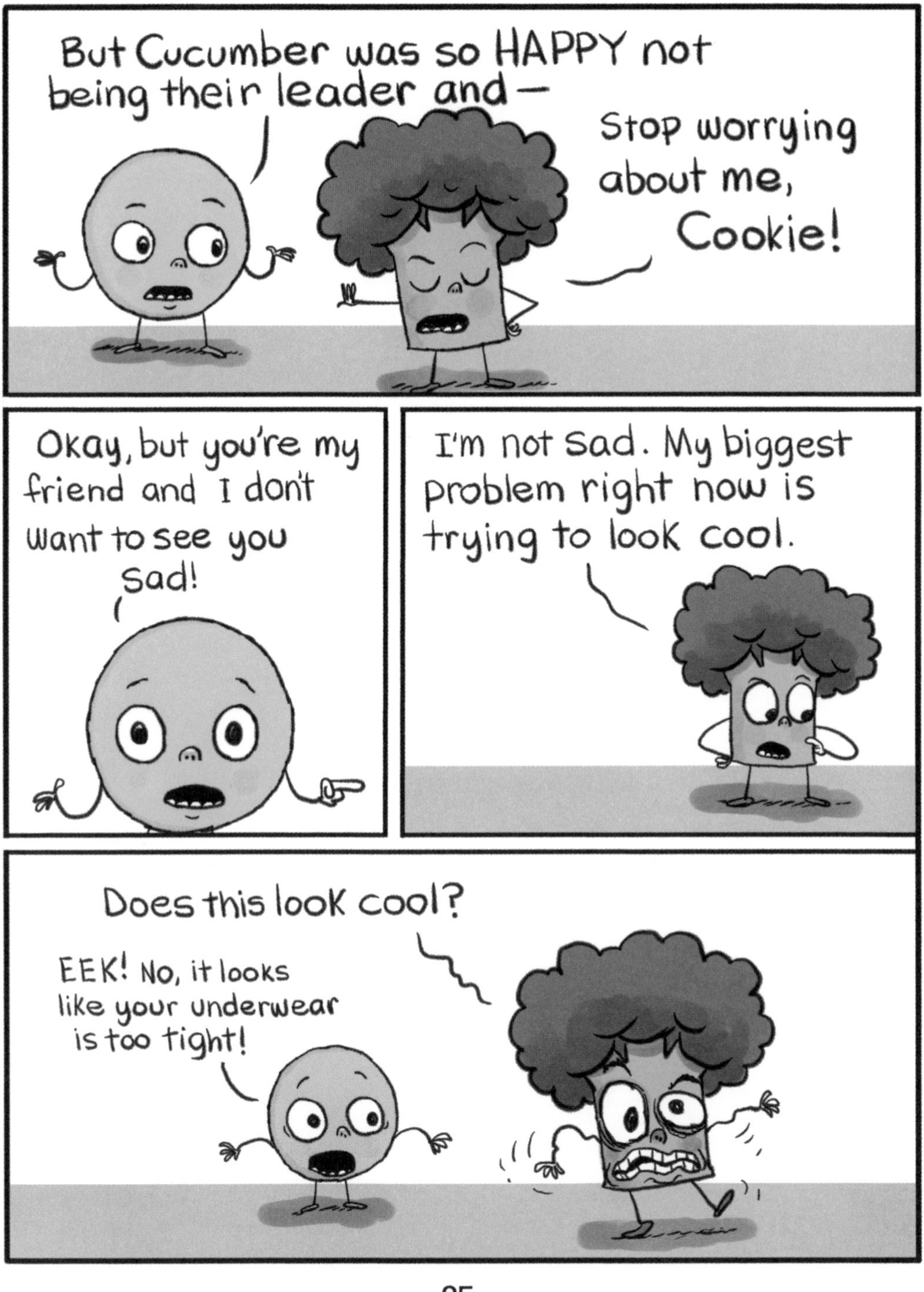
But Cucumber was so HAPPY not being their leader and—
Stop worrying about me, Cookie!
Okay, but you're my friend and I don't want to see you sad!
I'm not sad. My biggest problem right now is trying to look cool.
Does this look cool?
EEK! No, it looks like your underwear is too tight!

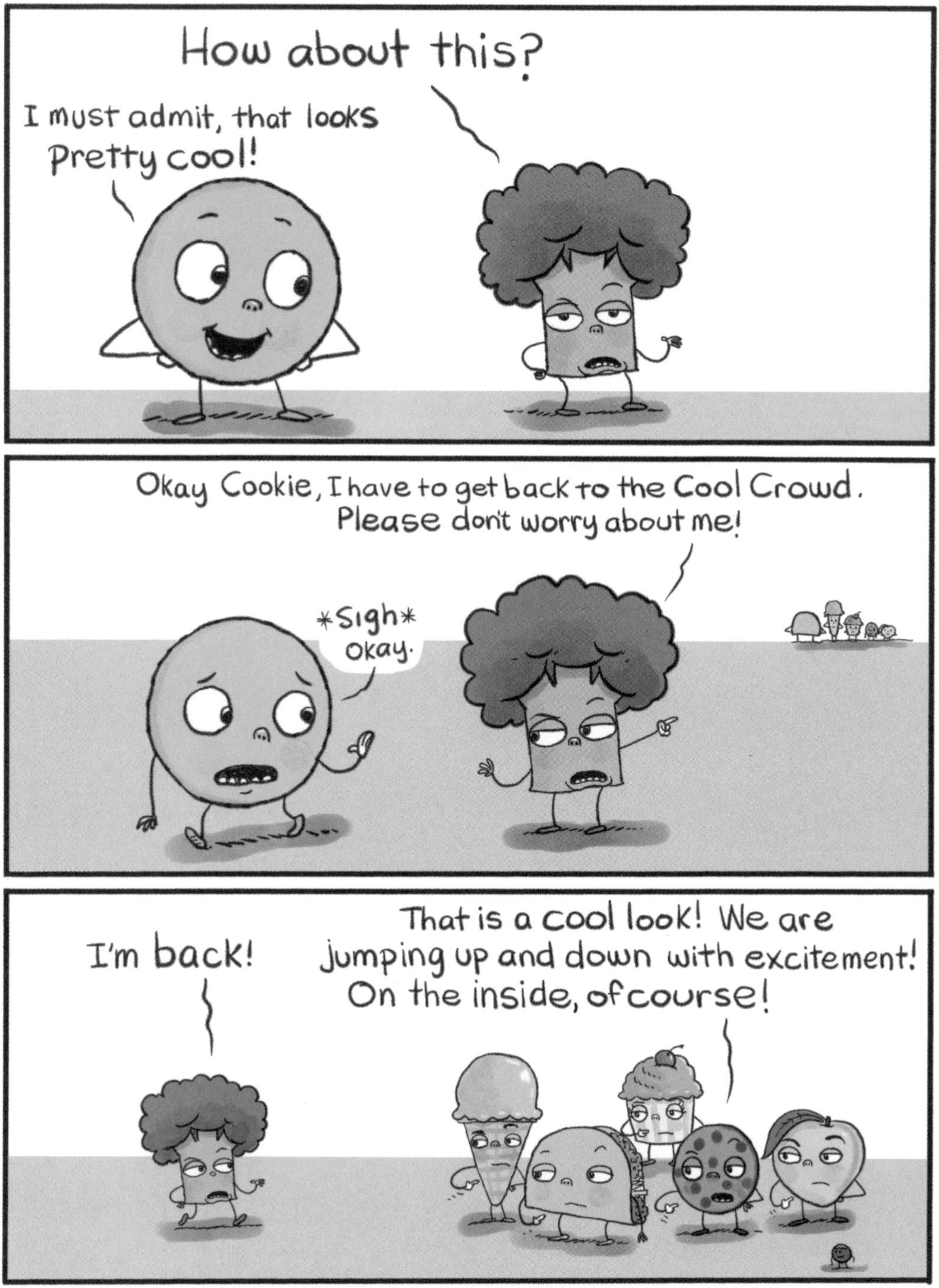
How about this?
I must admit, that looks pretty cool!
Okay Cookie, I have to get back to the Cool Crowd. Please don't worry about me!
Sigh okay.
I'm back!
That is a cool look! We are jumping up and down with excitement! On the inside, of course!

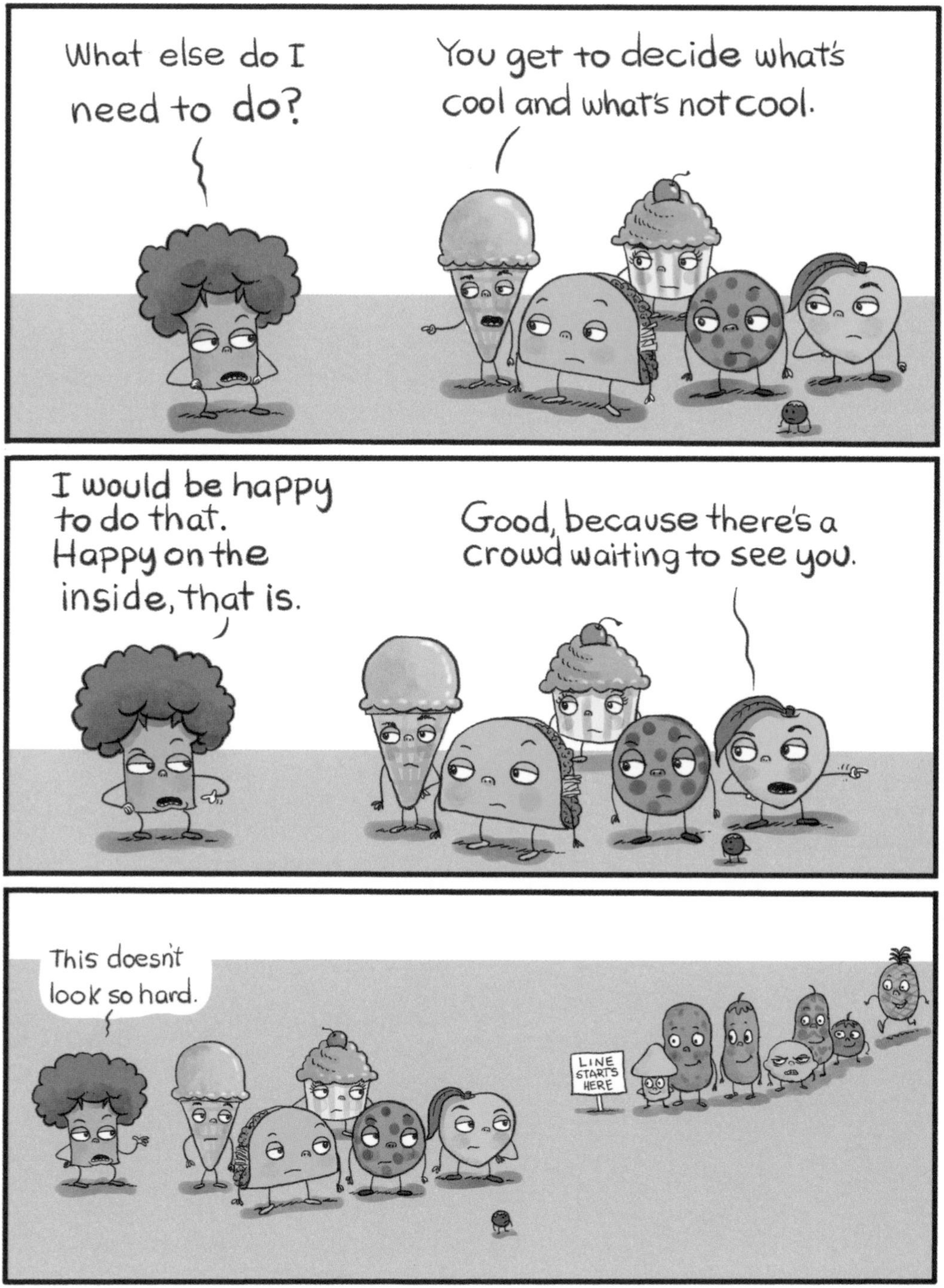
What else do I need to do?
You get to decide what's cool and what's not cool.
I would be happy to do that. Happy on the inside, that is.
Good, because there's a crowd waiting to see you.
This doesn't look so hard.
LINE STARTS HERE

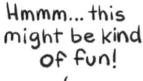
Hmmm... this might be kind of fun!

You may approach and ask your question!

Point Point

LINE STARTS HERE

Oh Cool Crowd leader, I am Mushroom. Am I cool even though I am just a fungi?

Yes, Mushroom, you ARE cool! In fact, mushrooms put the "fun" in fungus!

Thank you!

Next!

I got this green stuff between my toes. Is that cool?

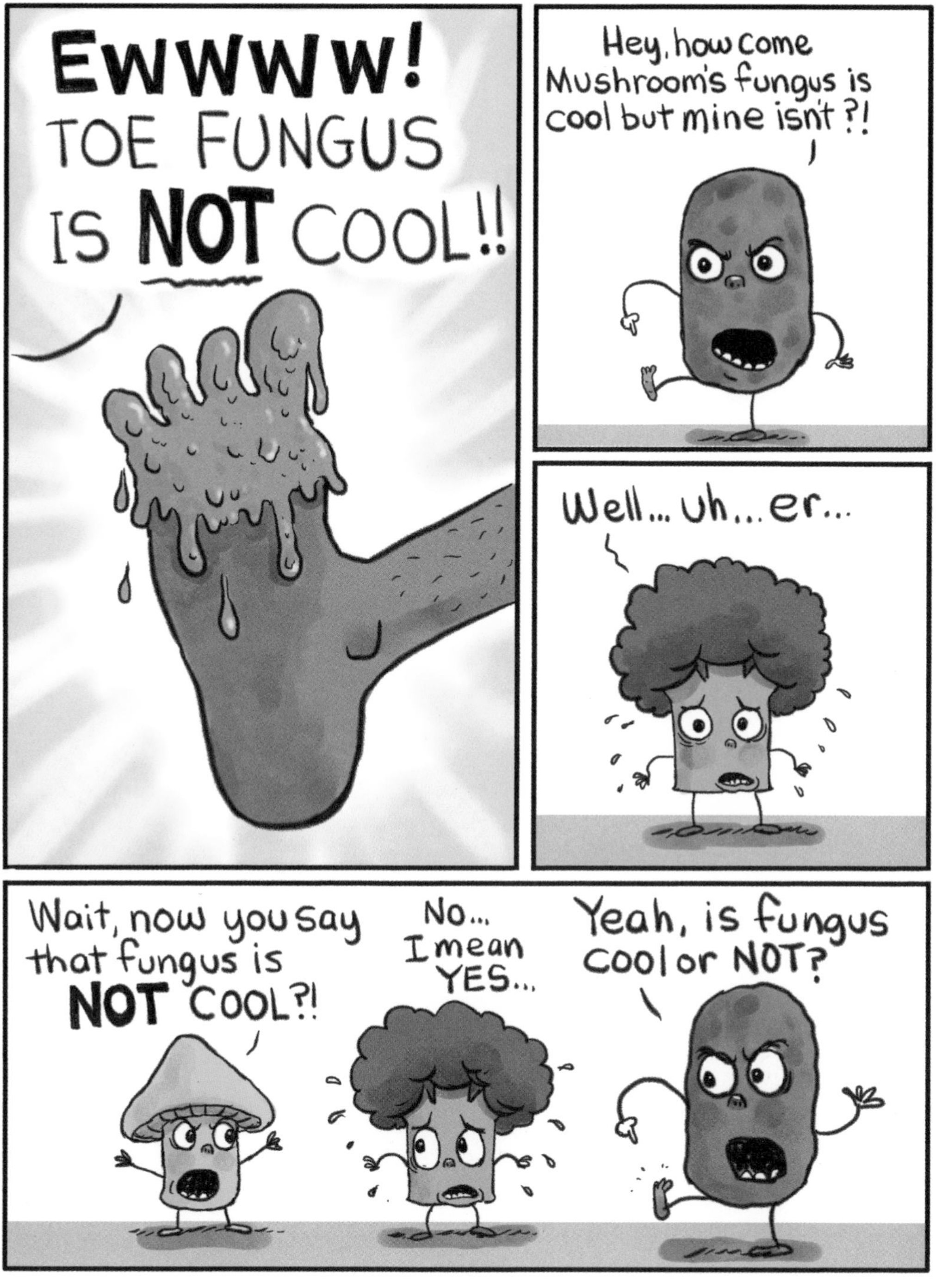
EWWWW! TOE FUNGUS IS NOT COOL!!
Hey, how come Mushroom's fungus is cool but mine isn't?!
Well... uh... er...
Wait, now you say that fungus is NOT COOL?!
No... I mean YES...
Yeah, is fungus cool or NOT?

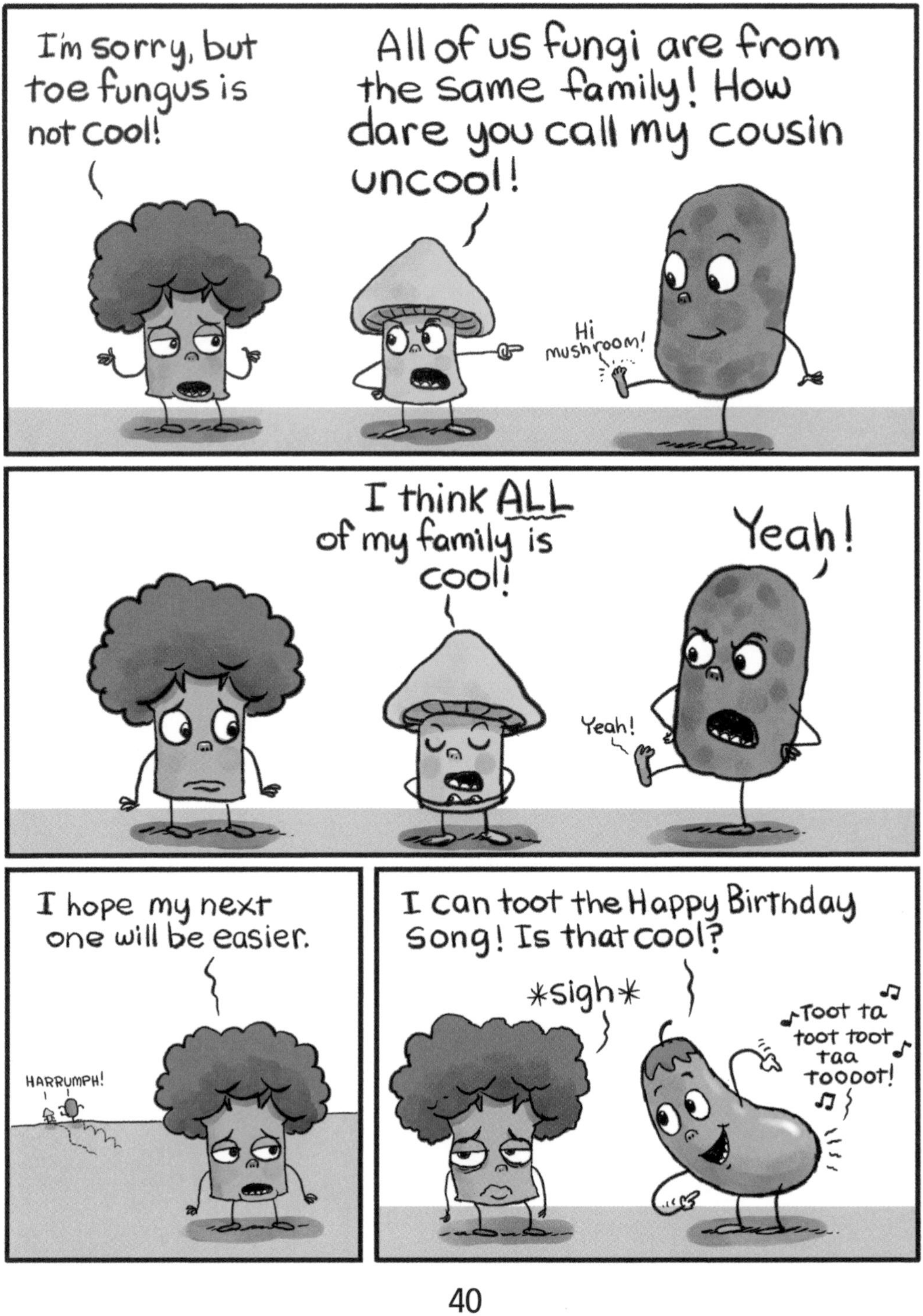
I'm sorry, but toe fungus is not cool!
All of us fungi are from the same family! How dare you call my cousin uncool!
Hi mushroom!
I think ALL of my family is cool!
Yeah!
Yeah!
I hope my next one will be easier.
HARRUMPH!
I can toot the Happy Birthday song! Is that cool?
sigh
Toot ta toot toot taa toooot!

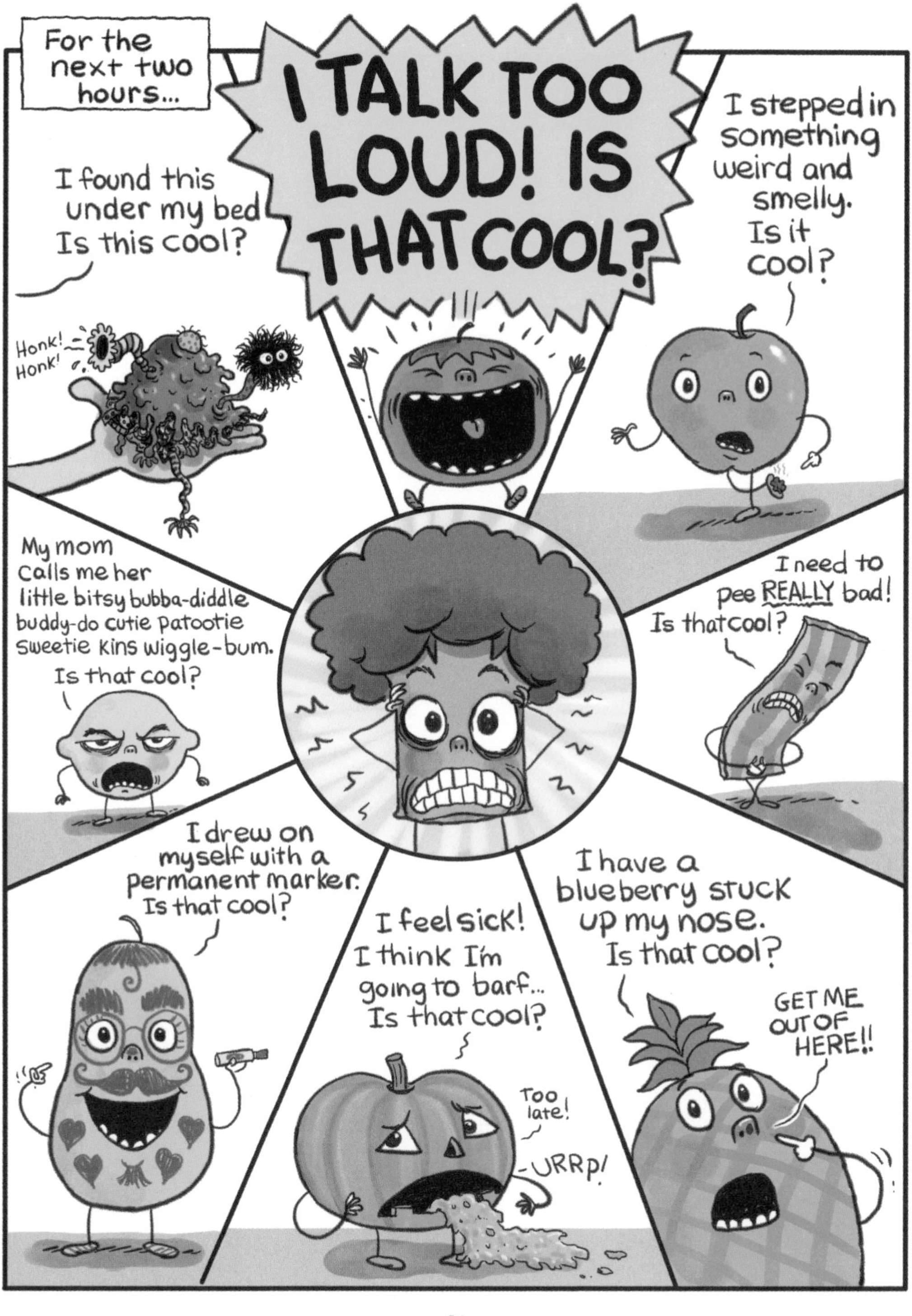
For the next two hours...
I TALK TOO LOUD! IS THAT COOL?
I found this under my bed Is this cool?
Honk! Honk!
I stepped in something weird and smelly. Is it cool?
My mom calls me her little bitsy bubba-diddle buddy-do cutie patootie sweetie kins wiggle-bum. Is that cool?
I need to pee REALLY bad! Is that cool?
I drew on myself with a permanent marker. Is that cool?
I feel sick! I think I'm going to barf... Is that cool?
Too late!
-URRP!
I have a blueberry stuck up my nose. Is that cool?
GET ME OUT OF HERE!!

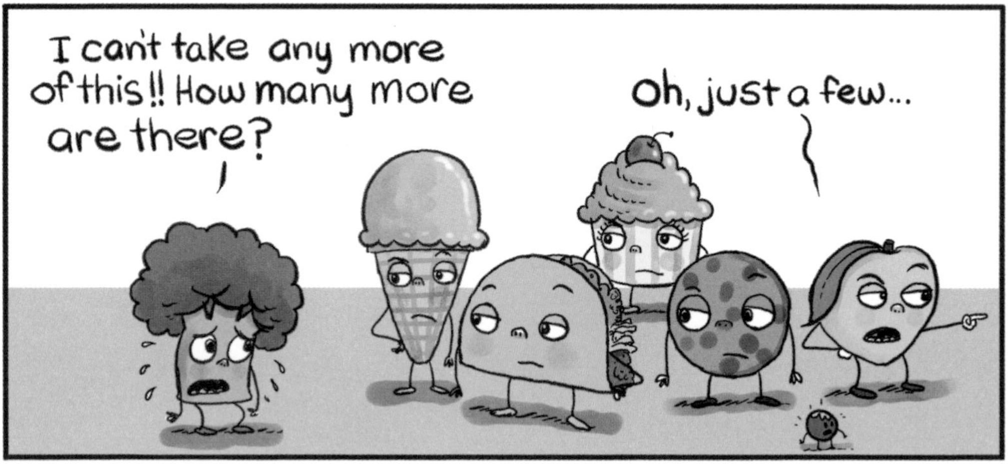
I can't take any more of this!! How many more are there?
Oh, just a few...

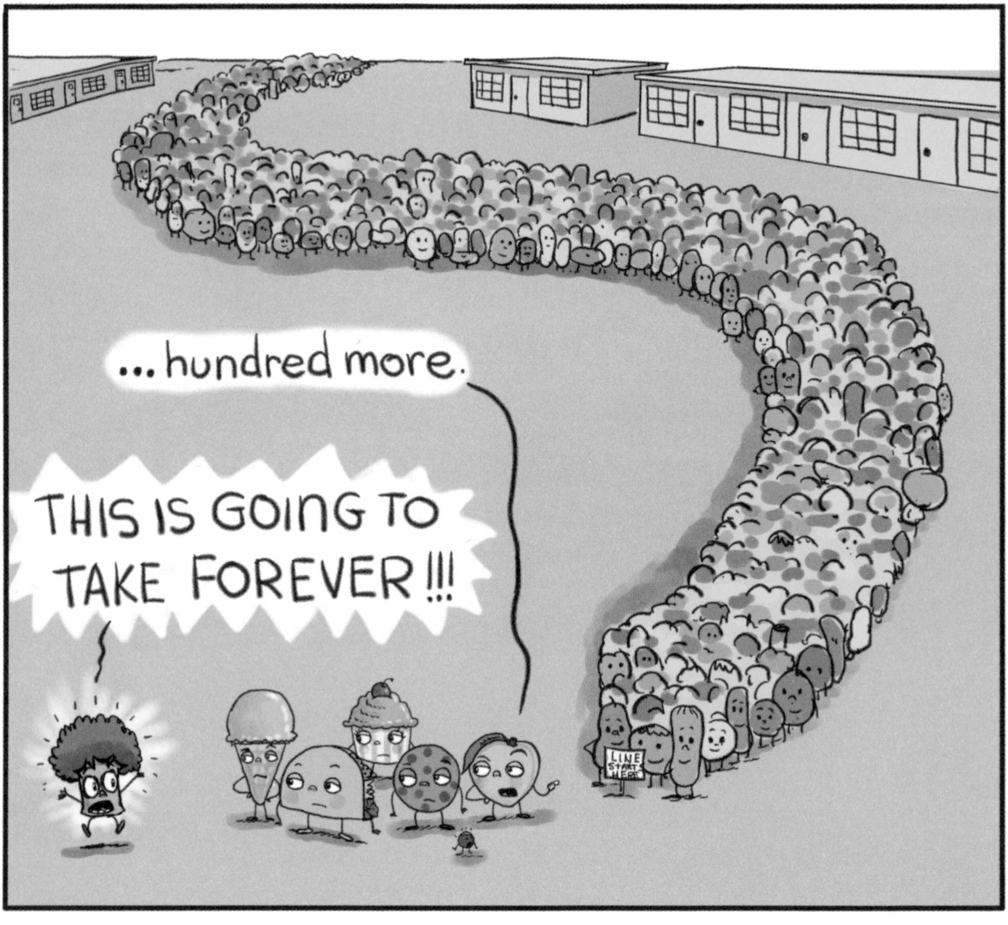
...hundred more.
THIS IS GOING TO TAKE FOREVER!!!
LINE STARTS HERE

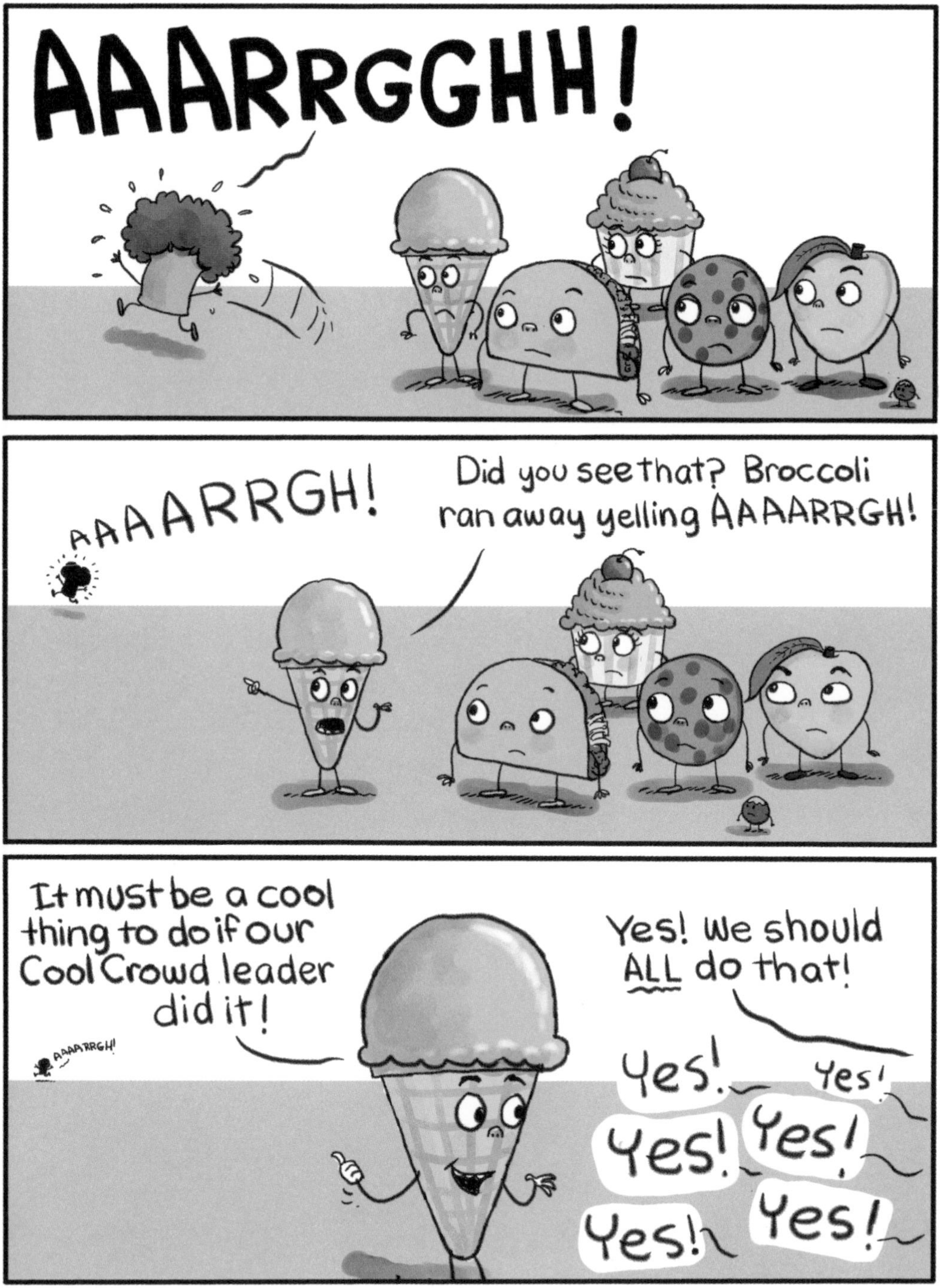
AAARRGGHH!
AAAARRRGH!
Did you see that? Broccoli ran away yelling AAAARRGH!
It must be a cool thing to do if our Cool Crowd leader did it!
AAAARRGH!
Yes! We should ALL do that!
Yes!
Yes!
Yes!
Yes!
Yes!
Yes!

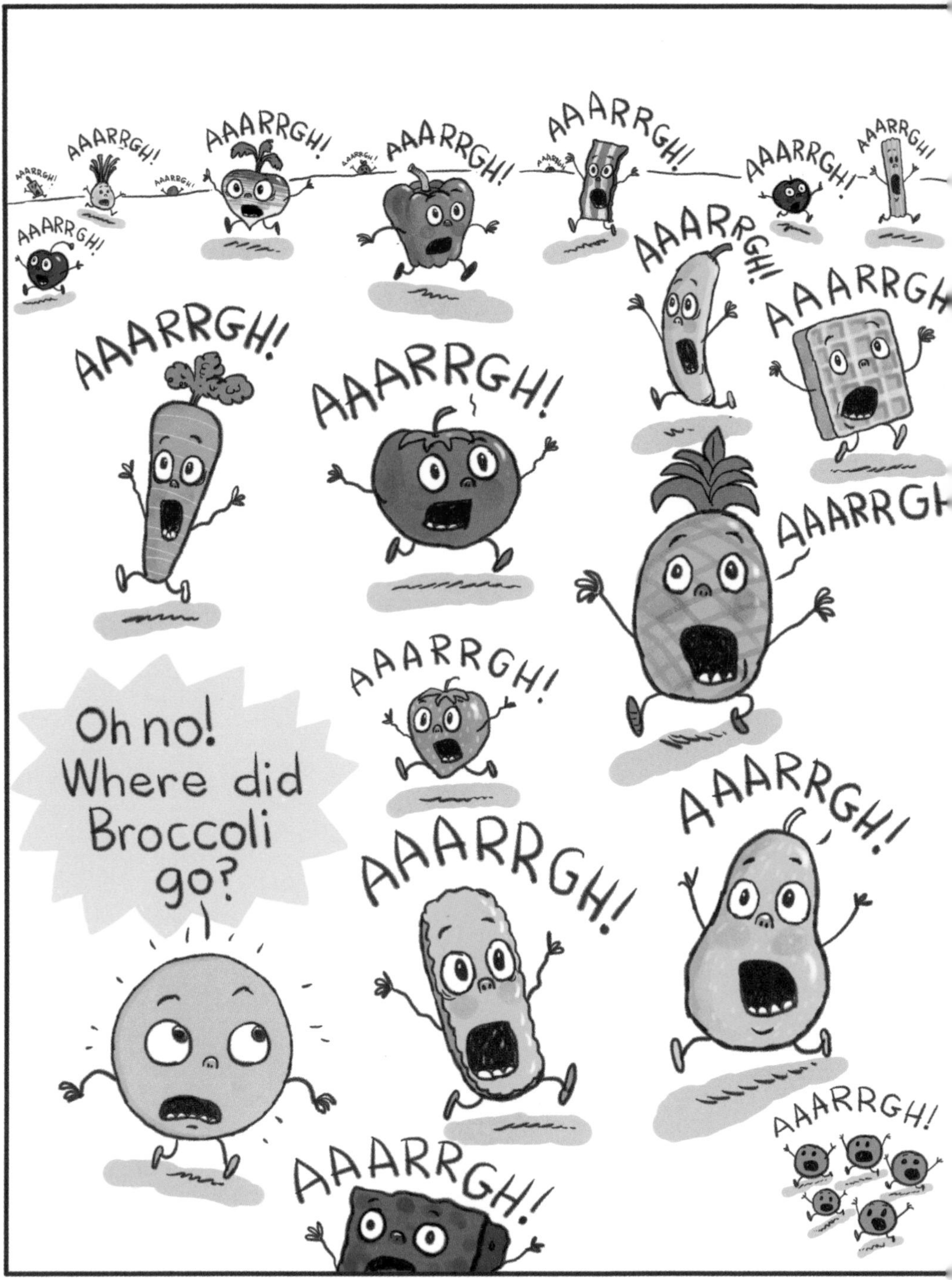
AAARRGH!
AAARRGH!
AAARRGH!
AAARRGH!
AAARRGH!
AAARRGH!
AAARRGH!
AAARRGH!
AAARRGH!
AAARRGH!
AAARRGH!
AAARRGH!
AAARRGH!
AAARRGH!
AAARRGH!
AAARRGH!
AAARRGH!
Oh no! Where did Broccoli go?
AAARRGH!
AAARRGH!
AAARRGH!

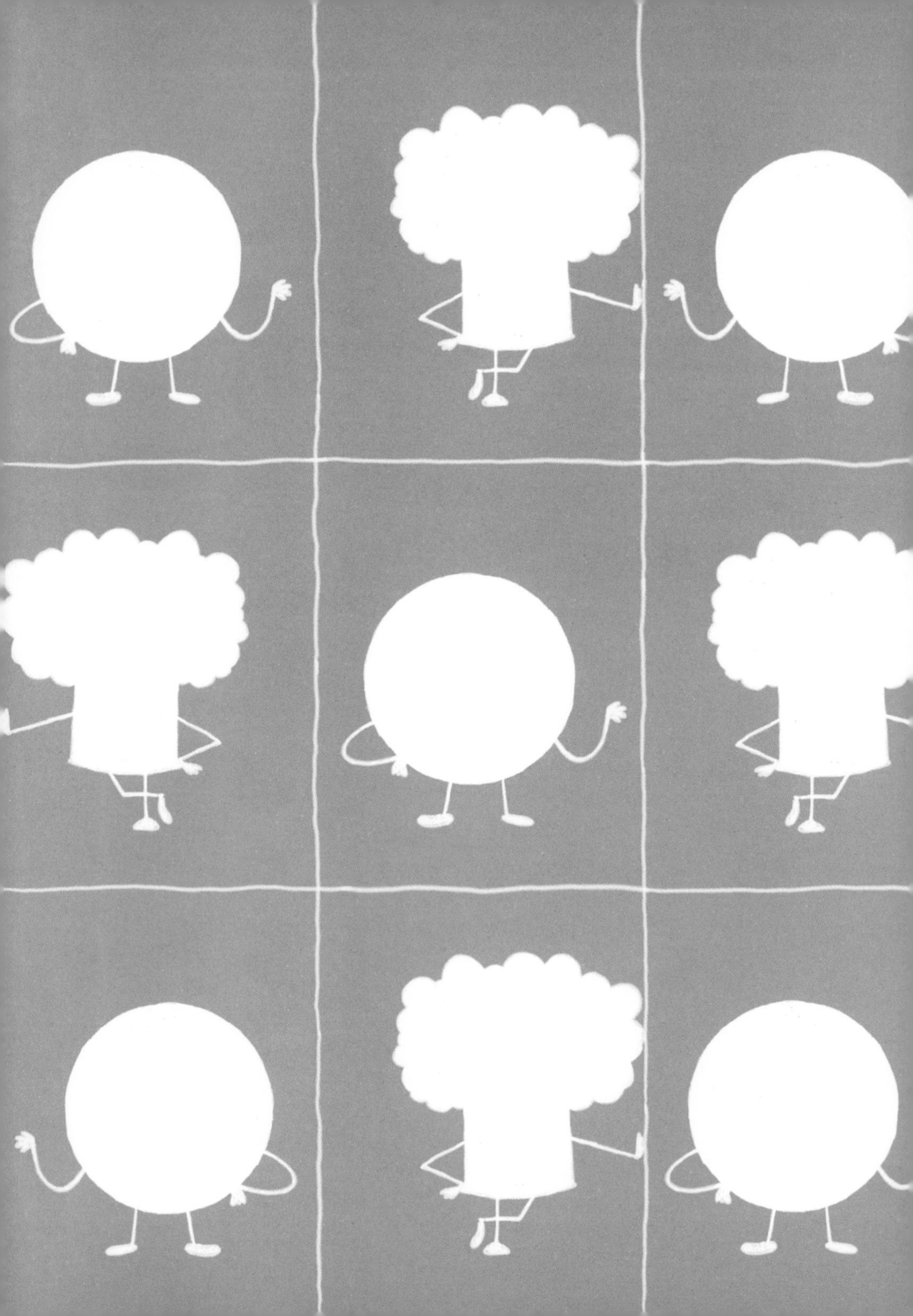

Chapter 3

BROCCOLI'S BIG ESCAPE!

Where did Broccoli go?

I'll never tell.

No one back here!

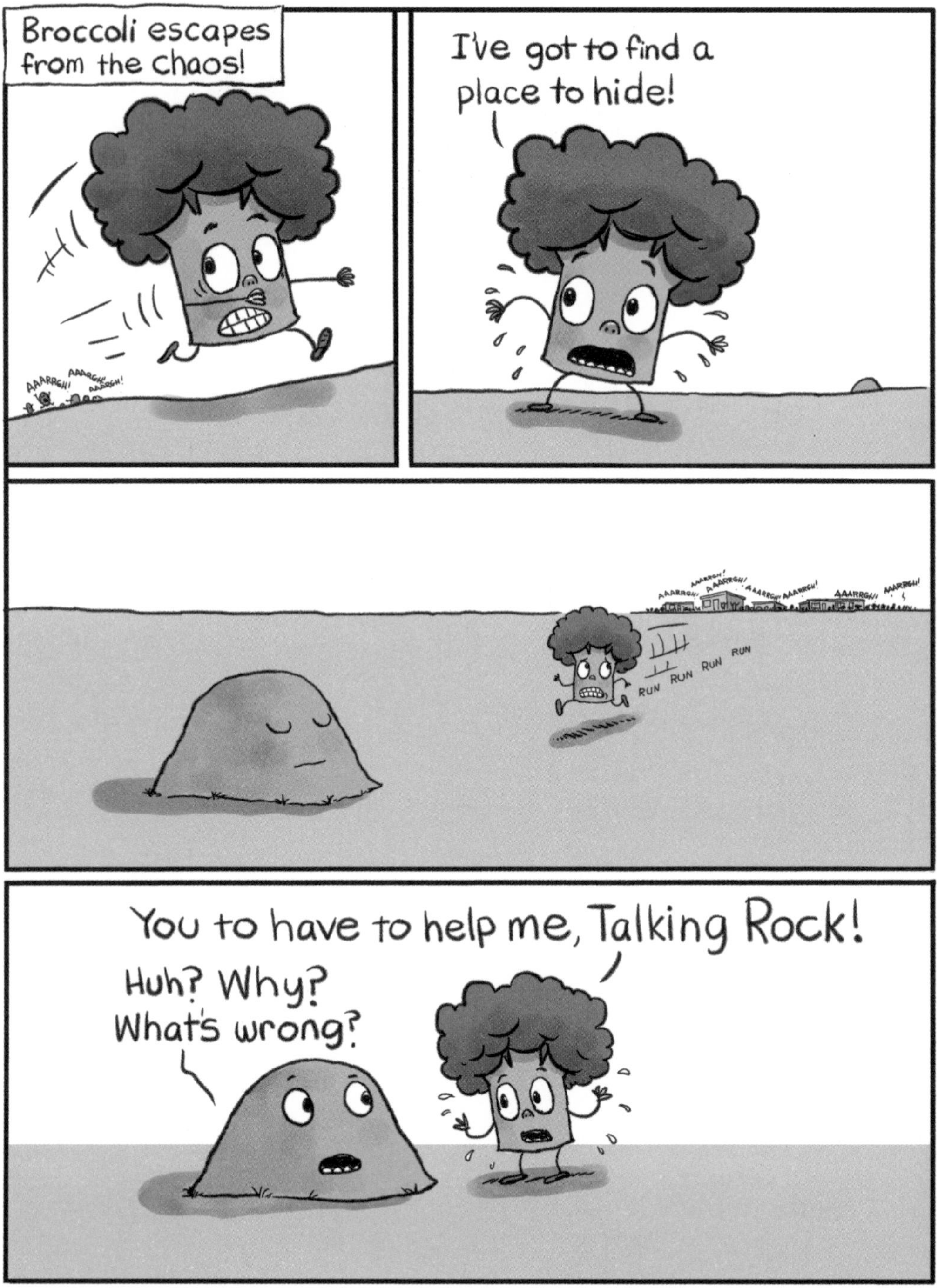
Broccoli escapes from the chaos!
I've got to find a place to hide!
RUN RUN RUN RUN
You to have to help me, Talking Rock!
Huh? Why? What's wrong?

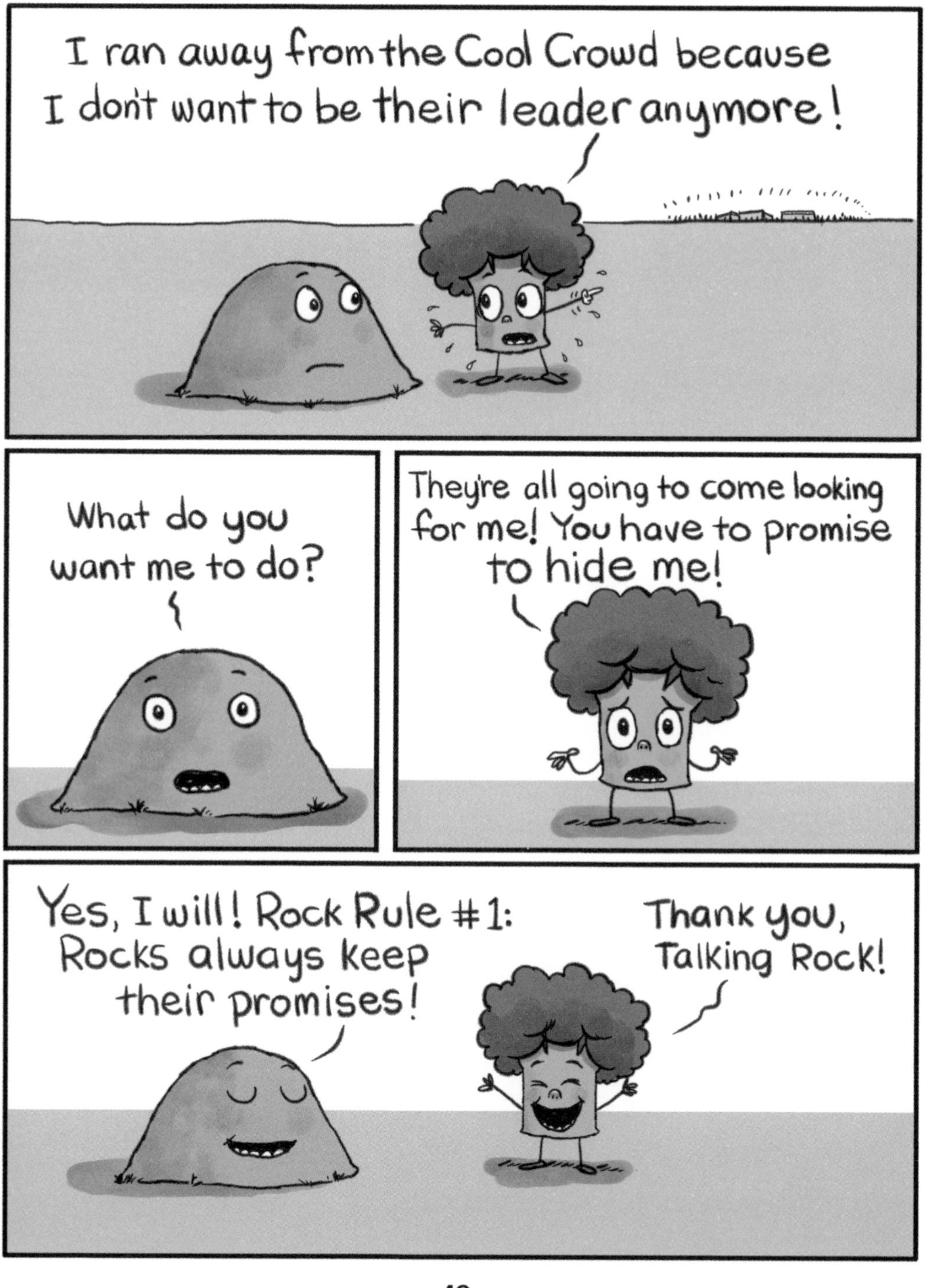
I ran away from the Cool Crowd because I don't want to be their leader anymore!
What do you want me to do?
They're all going to come looking for me! You have to promise to hide me!
Yes, I will! Rock Rule #1: Rocks always keep their promises!
Thank you, Talking Rock!

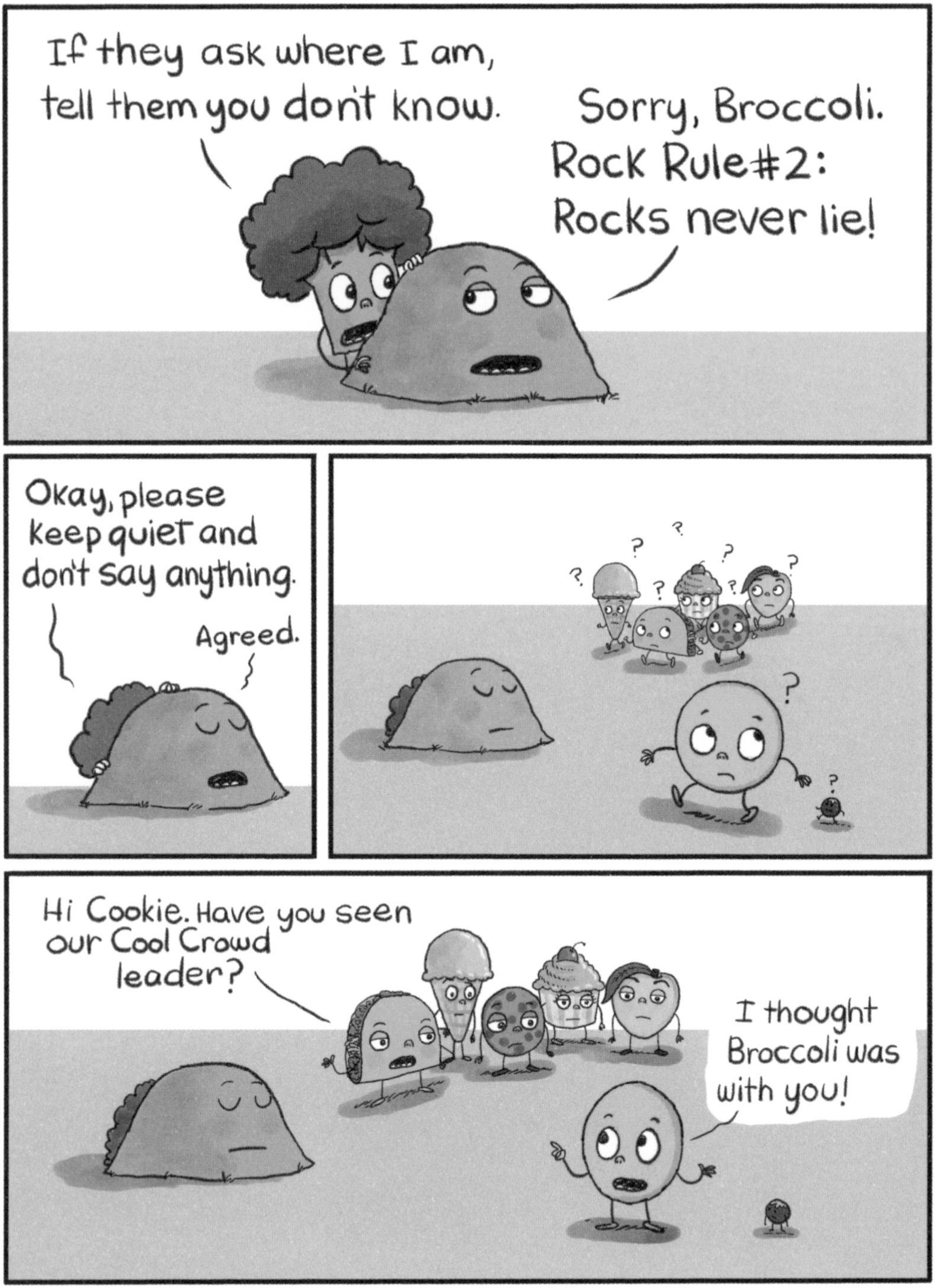
If they ask where I am, tell them you don't know.
Sorry, Broccoli. Rock Rule #2: Rocks never lie!
Okay, please keep quiet and don't say anything.
Agreed.
Hi Cookie. Have you seen our Cool Crowd leader?
I thought Broccoli was with you!

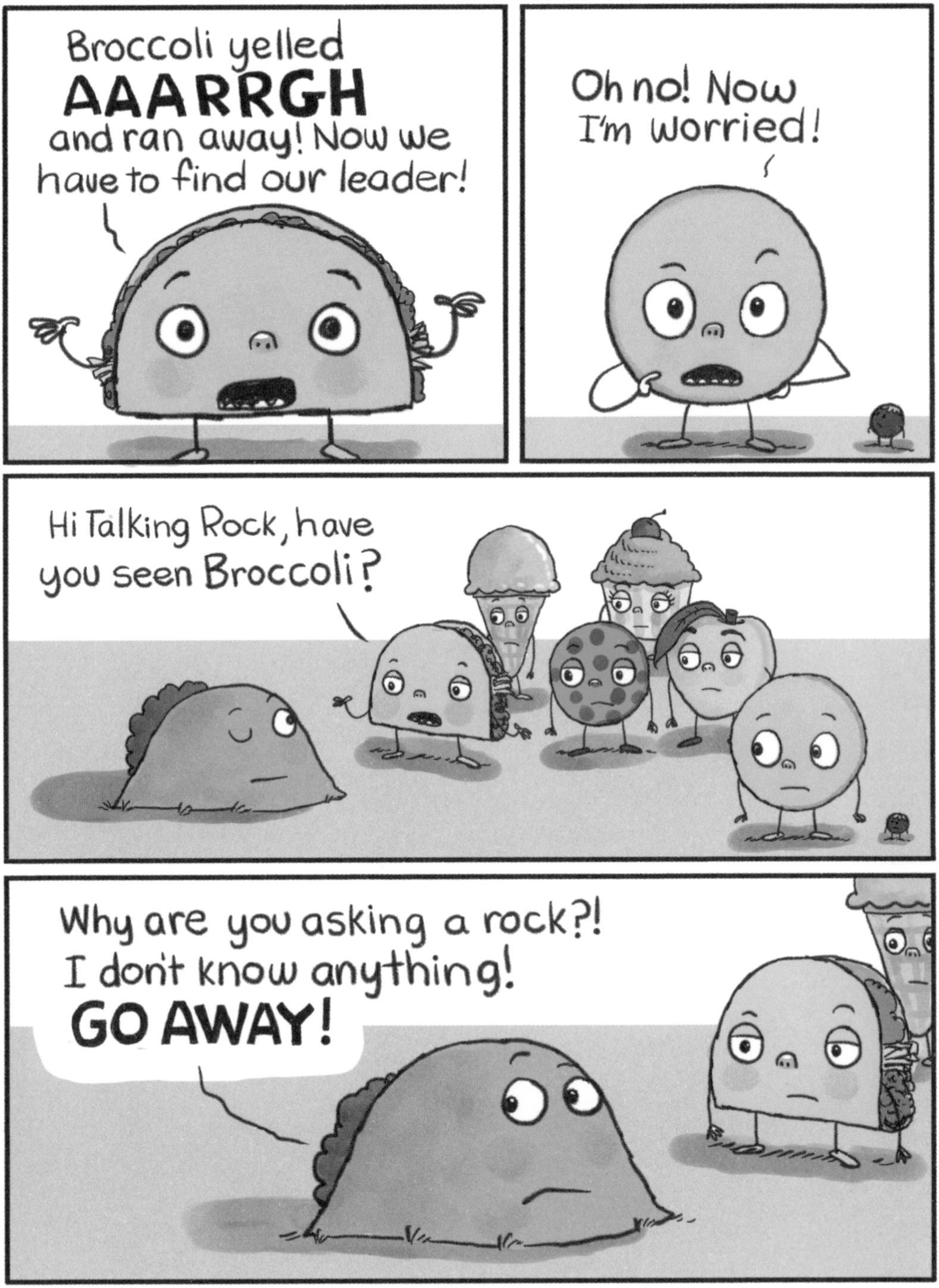
Broccoli yelled
AAARRGH
and ran away! Now we have to find our leader!
Oh no! Now I'm worried!
Hi Talking Rock, have you seen Broccoli?
Why are you asking a rock?! I don't know anything!
GO AWAY!

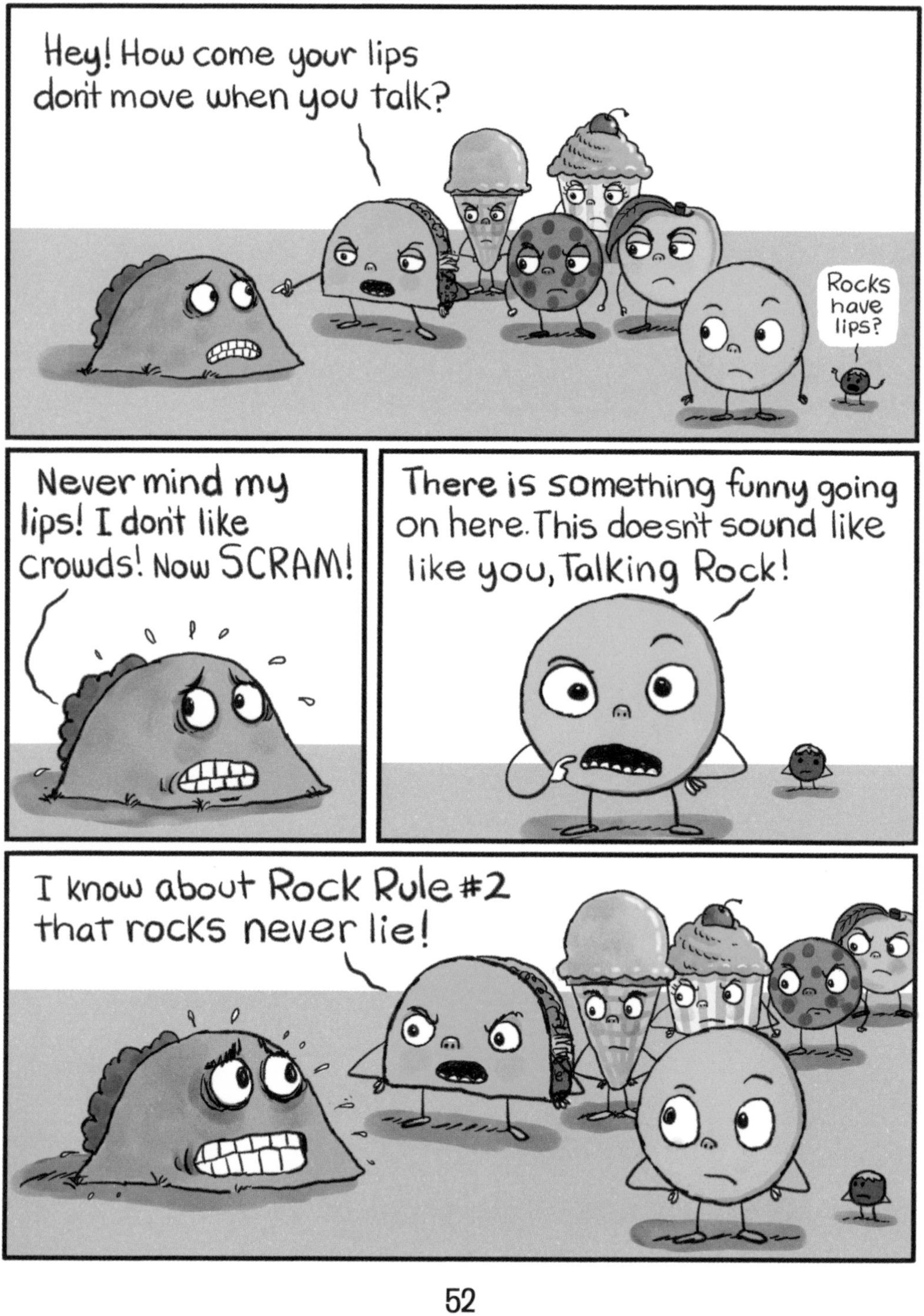
Hey! How come your lips don't move when you talk?
Rocks have lips?
Never mind my lips! I don't like crowds! Now SCRAM!
There is something funny going on here. This doesn't sound like like you, Talking Rock!
I know about Rock Rule #2 that rocks never lie!

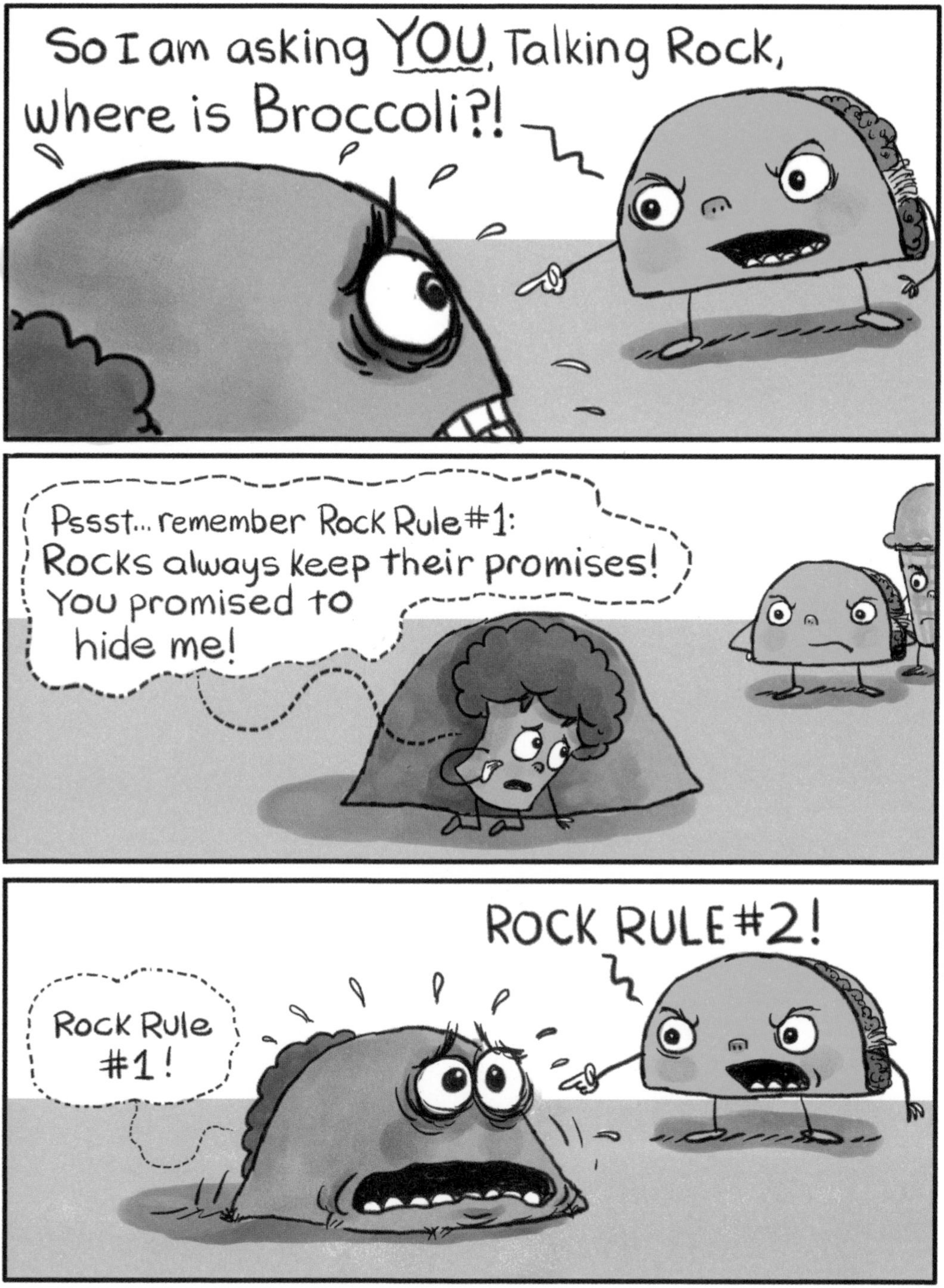
So I am asking YOU, Talking Rock, where is Broccoli?!
Pssst... remember Rock Rule #1: Rocks always keep their promises! You promised to hide me!
ROCK RULE #2!
Rock Rule #1!

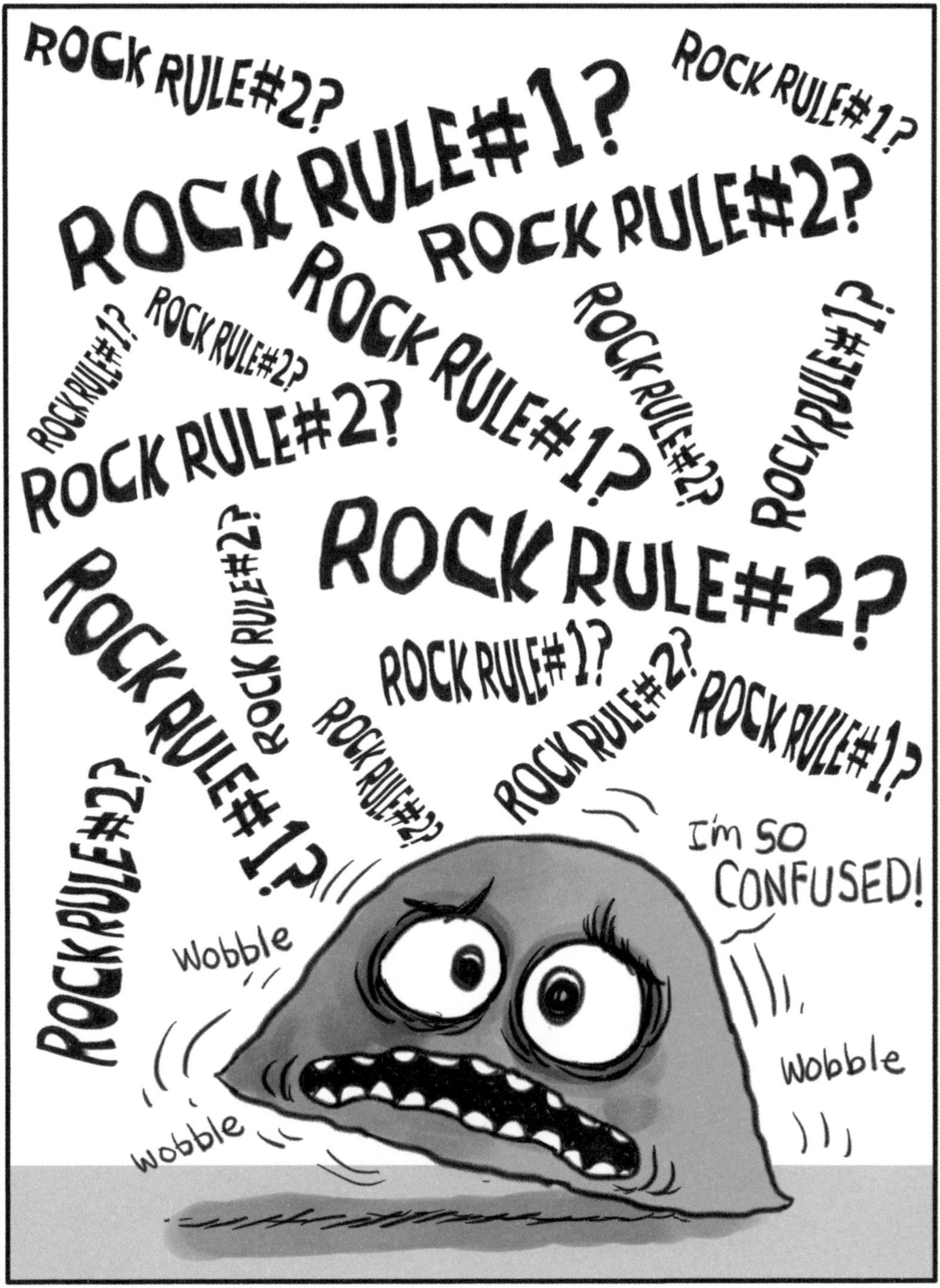
ROCK RULE#2?
ROCK RULE#1?
ROCK RULE#1?
ROCK RULE#2?
ROCK RULE#1?
ROCK RULE#2?
ROCK RULE#1?
ROCK RULE#2?
ROCK RULE#1?
ROCK RULE#2?
ROCK RULE#2?
ROCK RULE#1?
ROCK RULE#2?
ROCK RULE#1?
ROCK RULE#2?
ROCK RULE#1?
ROCK RULE#2?
ROCK RULE#2?
I'm SO CONFUSED!
Wobble
wobble
wobble

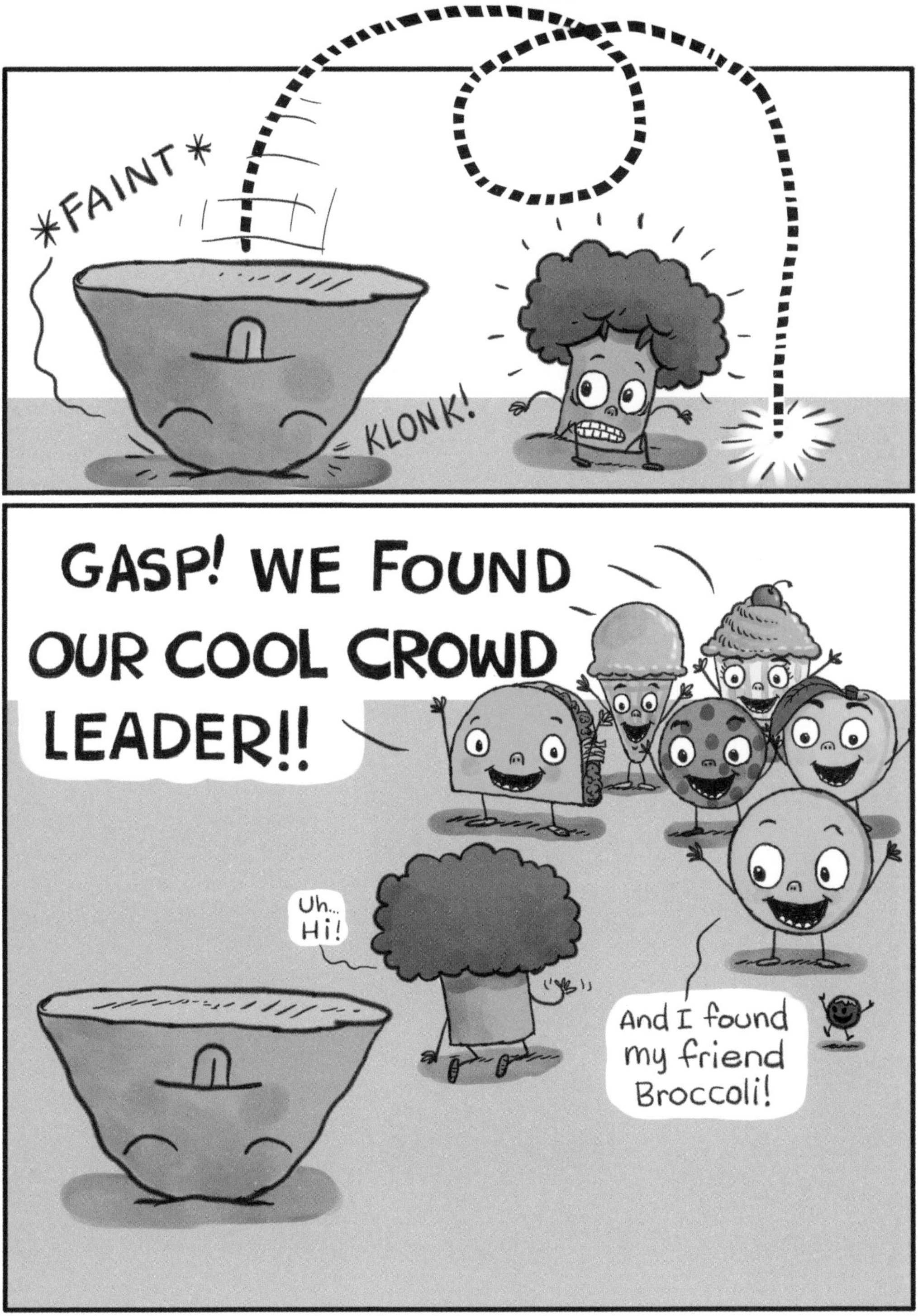
FAINT
KLONK!
GASP! WE FOUND OUR COOL CROWD LEADER!!
Uh... Hi!
And I found my friend Broccoli!

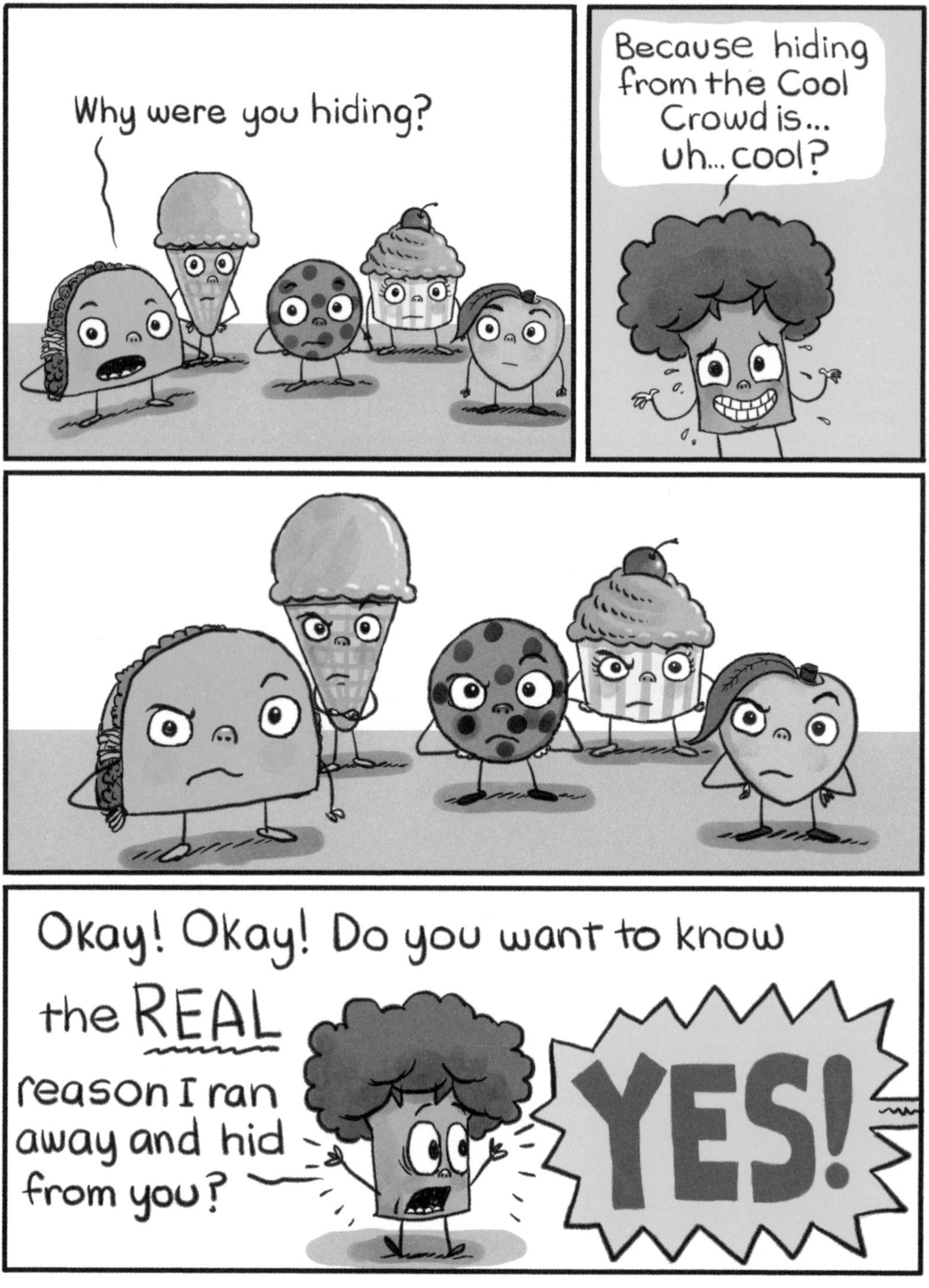

Why were you hiding?
Because hiding from the Cool Crowd is... uh... cool?
Okay! Okay! Do you want to know the REAL reason I ran away and hid from you?
YES!

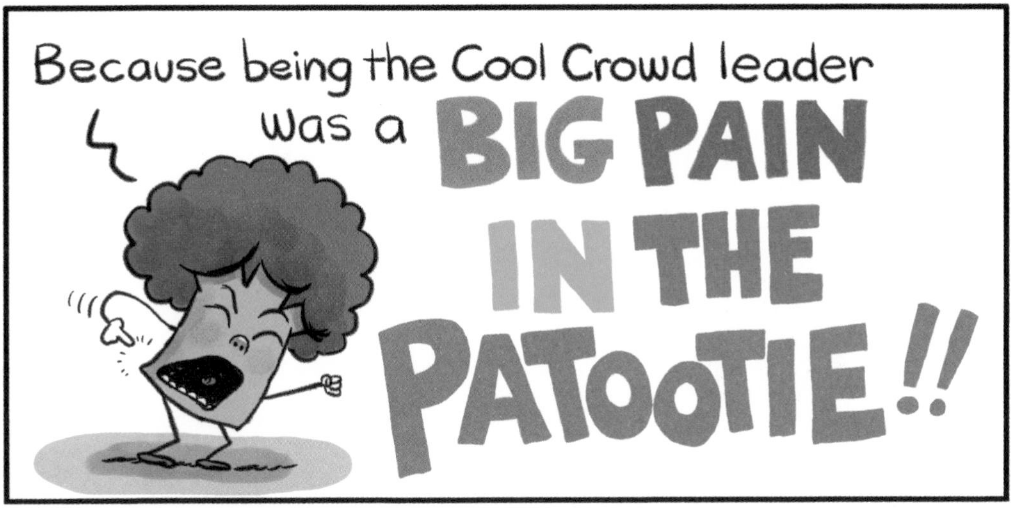
Because being the Cool Crowd leader was a BIG PAIN IN THE PATOOTIE!!

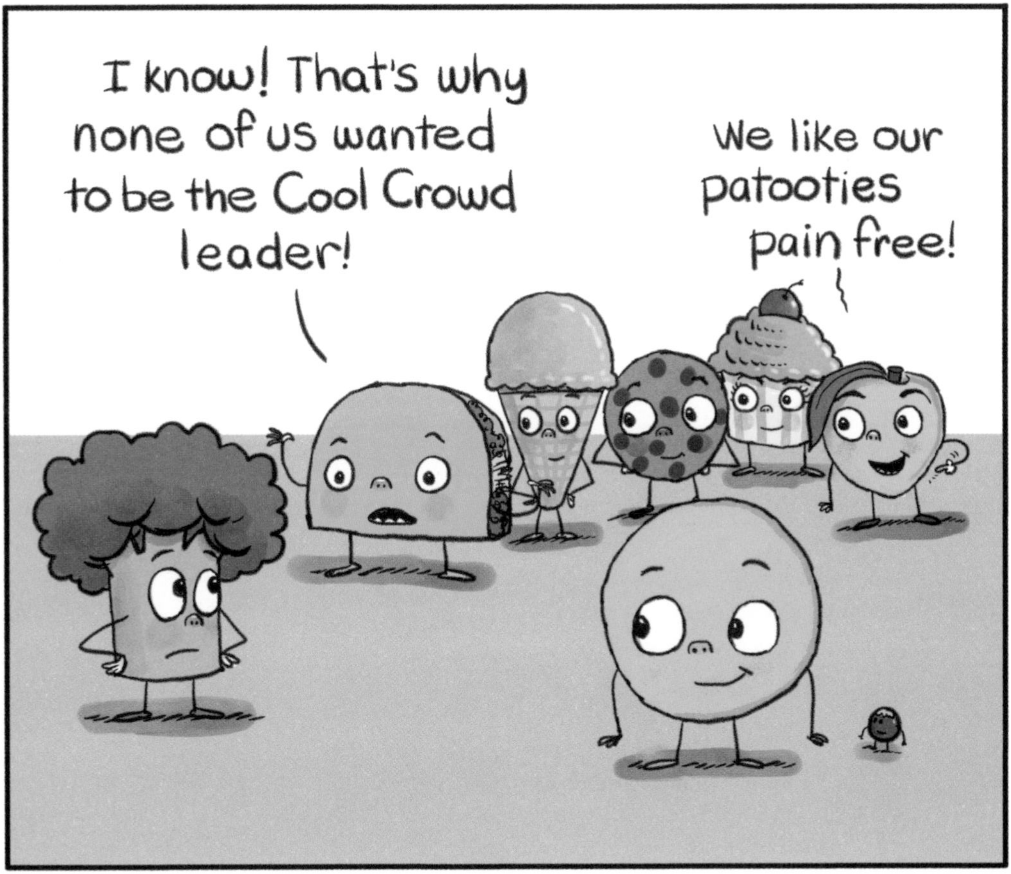
I know! That's why none of us wanted to be the Cool Crowd leader!
We like our patooties pain free!

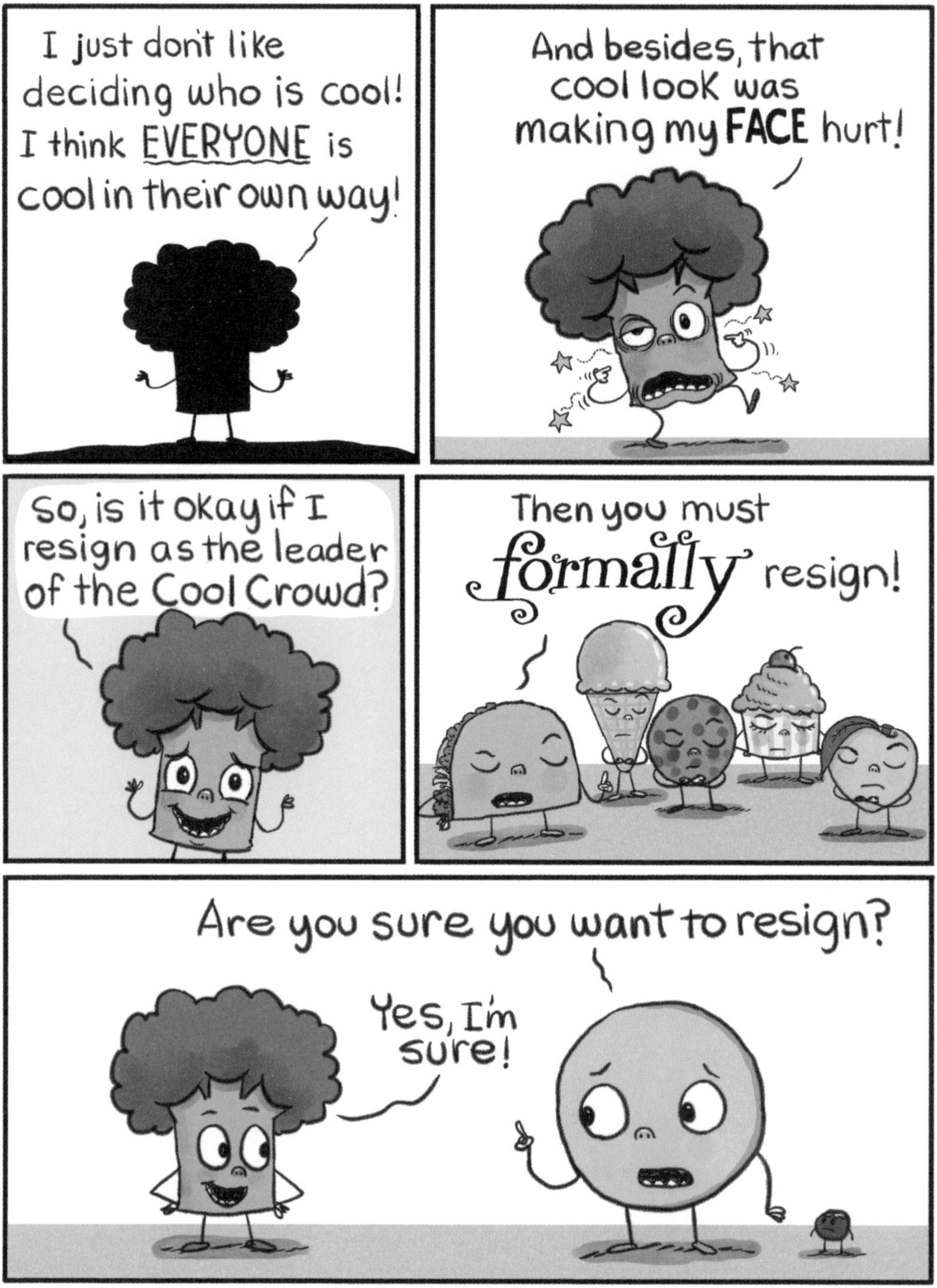
I just don't like deciding who is cool! I think EVERYONE is cool in their own way!
And besides, that cool look was making my FACE hurt!
So, is it okay if I resign as the leader of the Cool Crowd?
Then you must formally resign!
Are you sure you want to resign?
Yes, I'm sure!

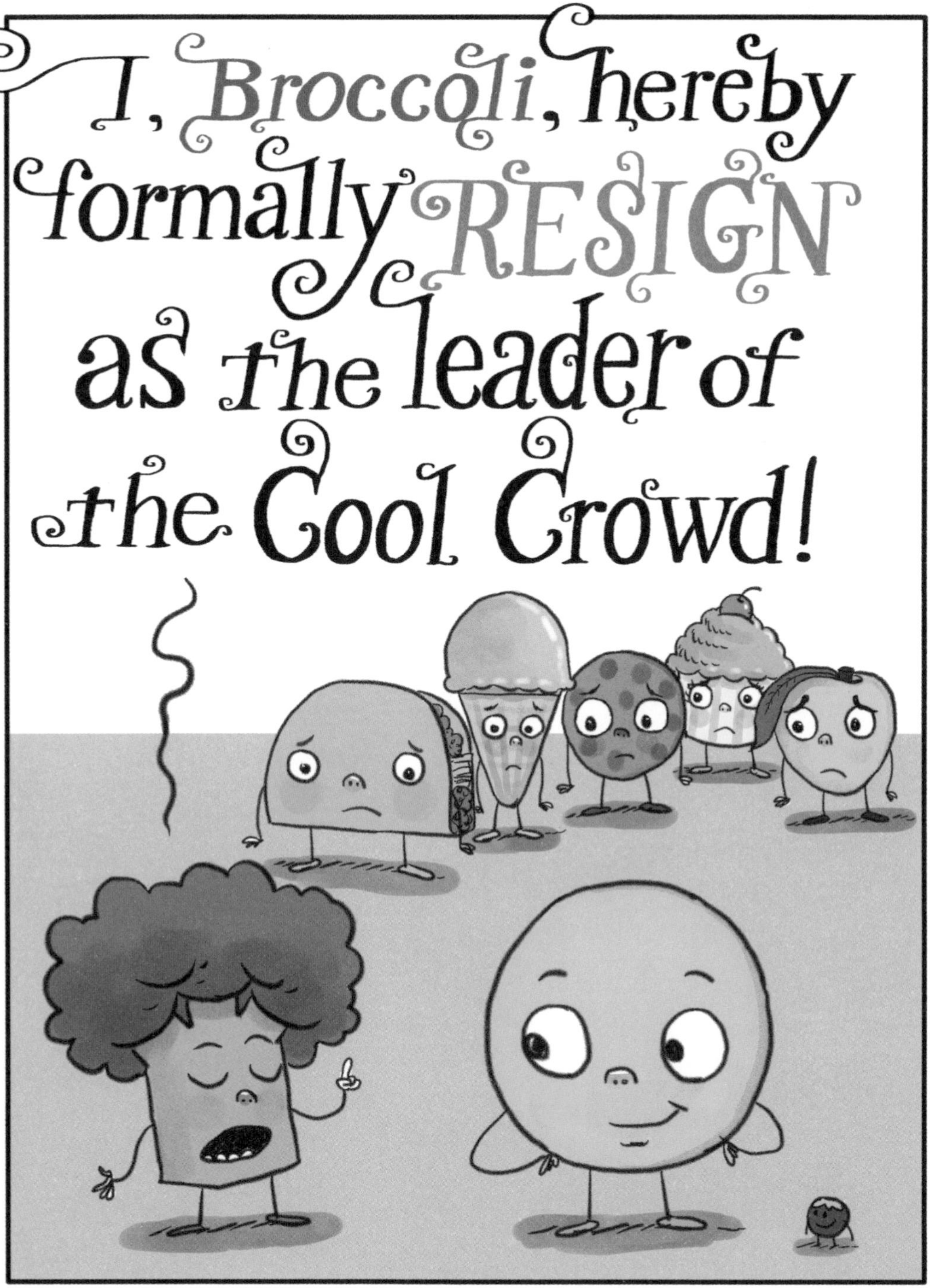
I, Broccoli, hereby formally RESIGN as the leader of the Cool Crowd!

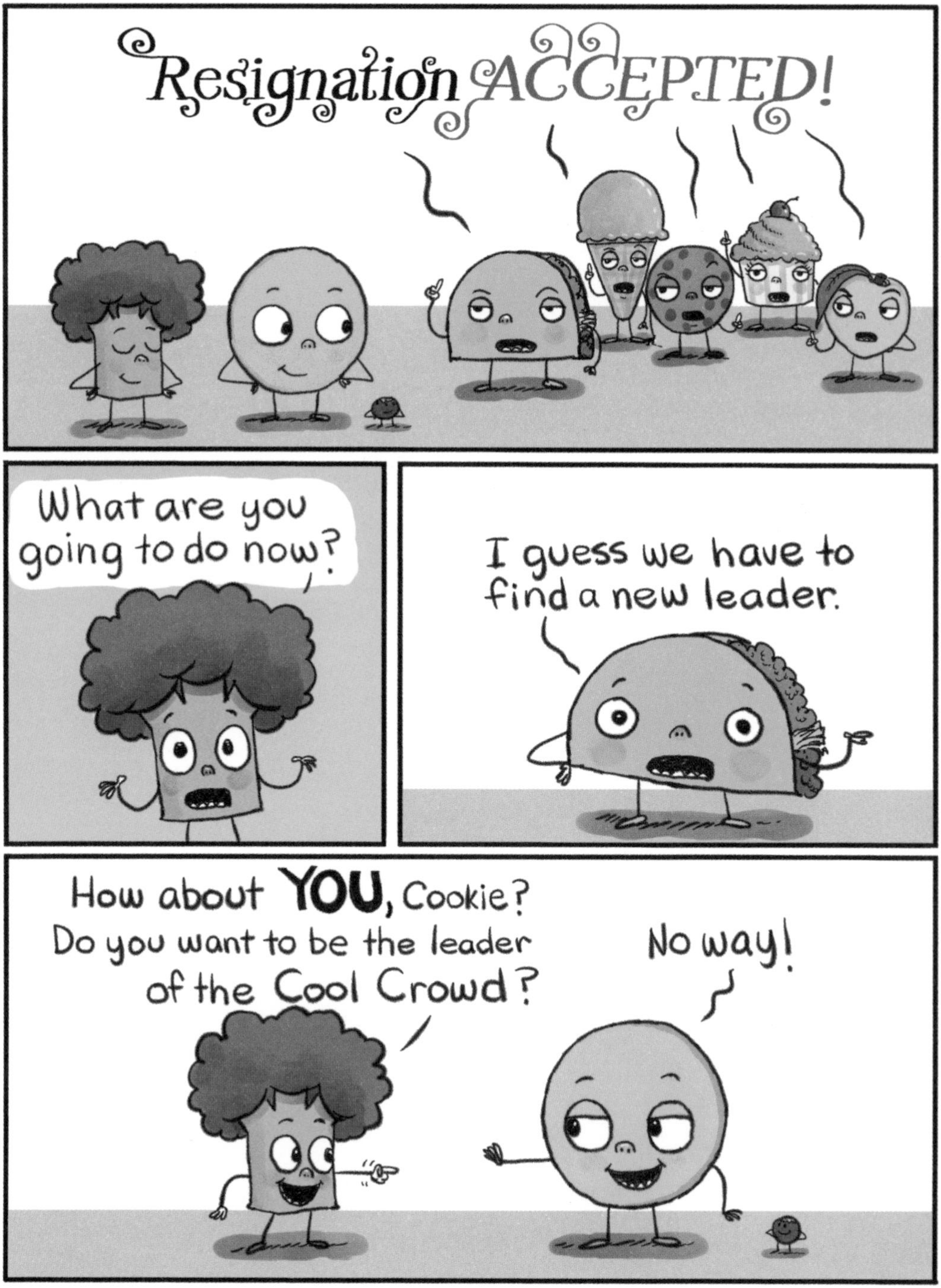
Resignation ACCEPTED!
What are you going to do now?
I guess we have to find a new leader.
How about YOU, Cookie? Do you want to be the leader of the Cool Crowd?
No way!

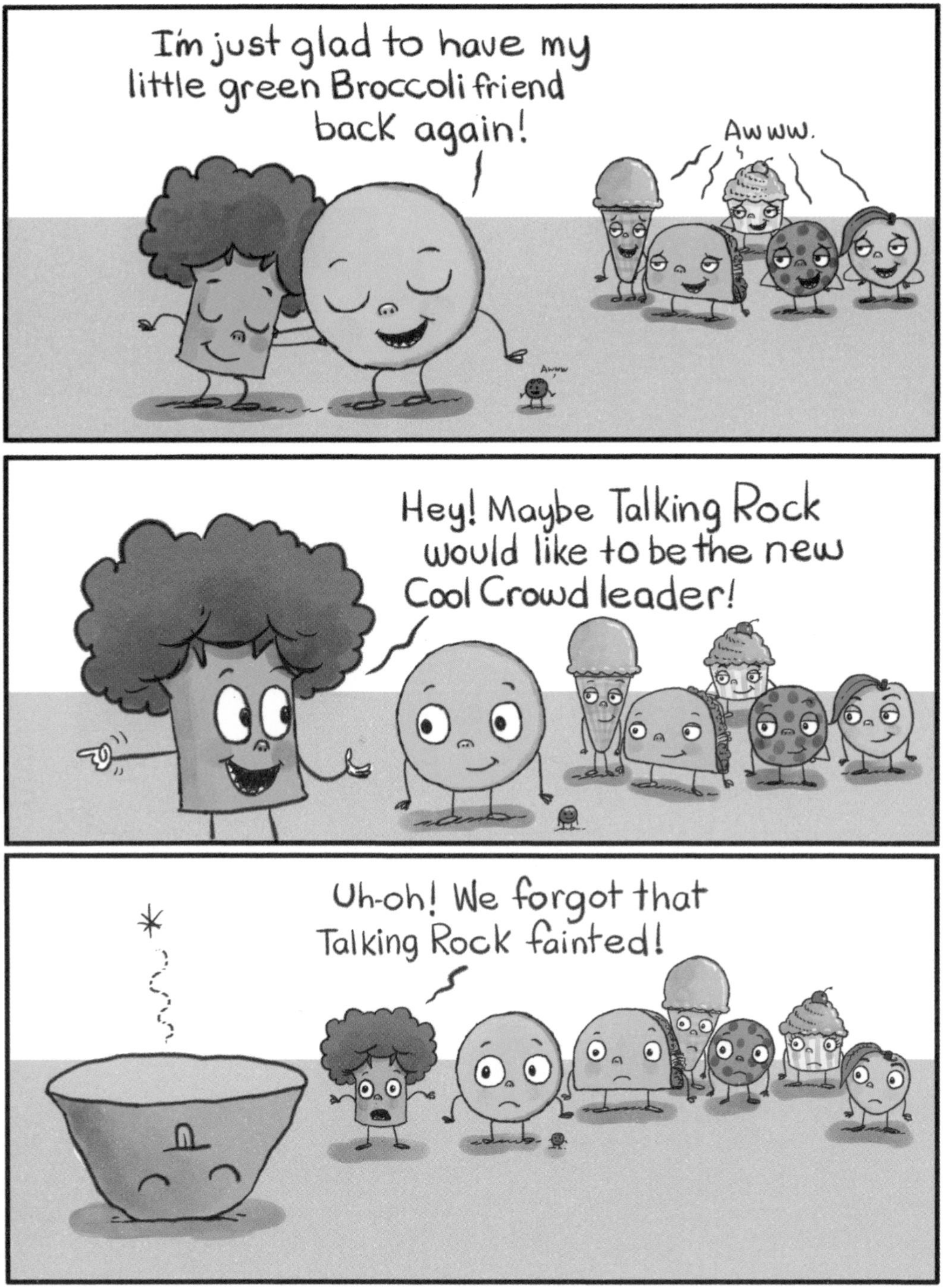

I'm just glad to have my little green Broccoli friend back again!
Awww.
Awww
Hey! Maybe Talking Rock would like to be the new Cool Crowd leader!
Uh-oh! We forgot that Talking Rock fainted!

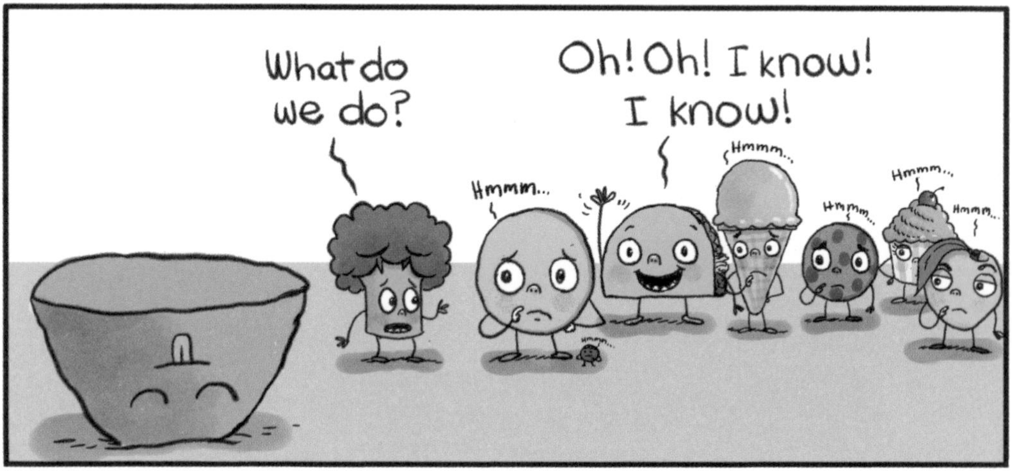
What do we do?
Hmmm...
Oh! Oh! I know! I know!
Hmmm...
Hmmm...
Hmmm...
Hmmm...

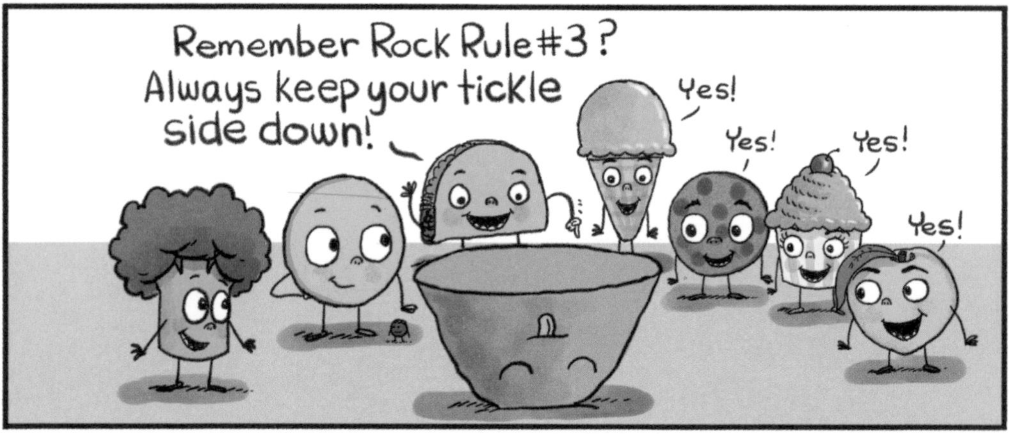
Remember Rock Rule #3? Always keep your tickle side down!
Yes!
Yes!
Yes!
Yes!

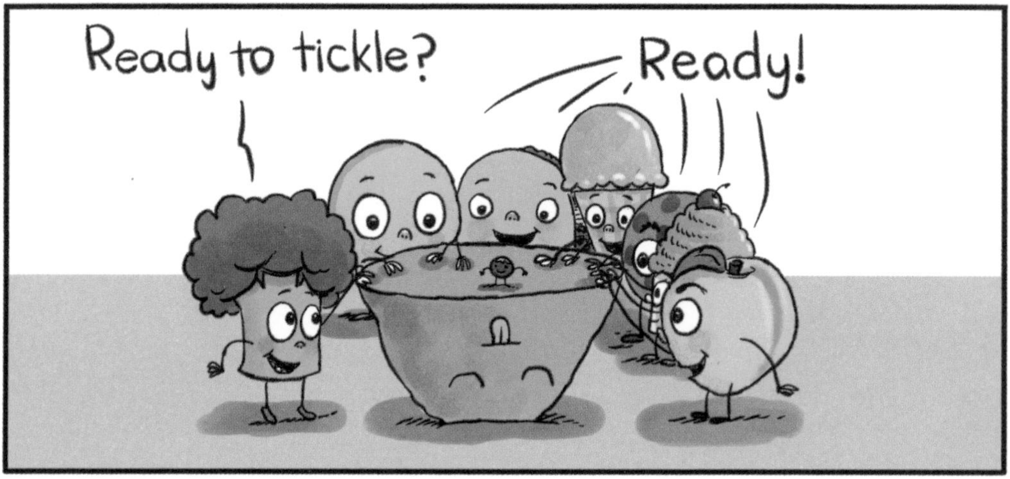
Ready to tickle?
Ready!

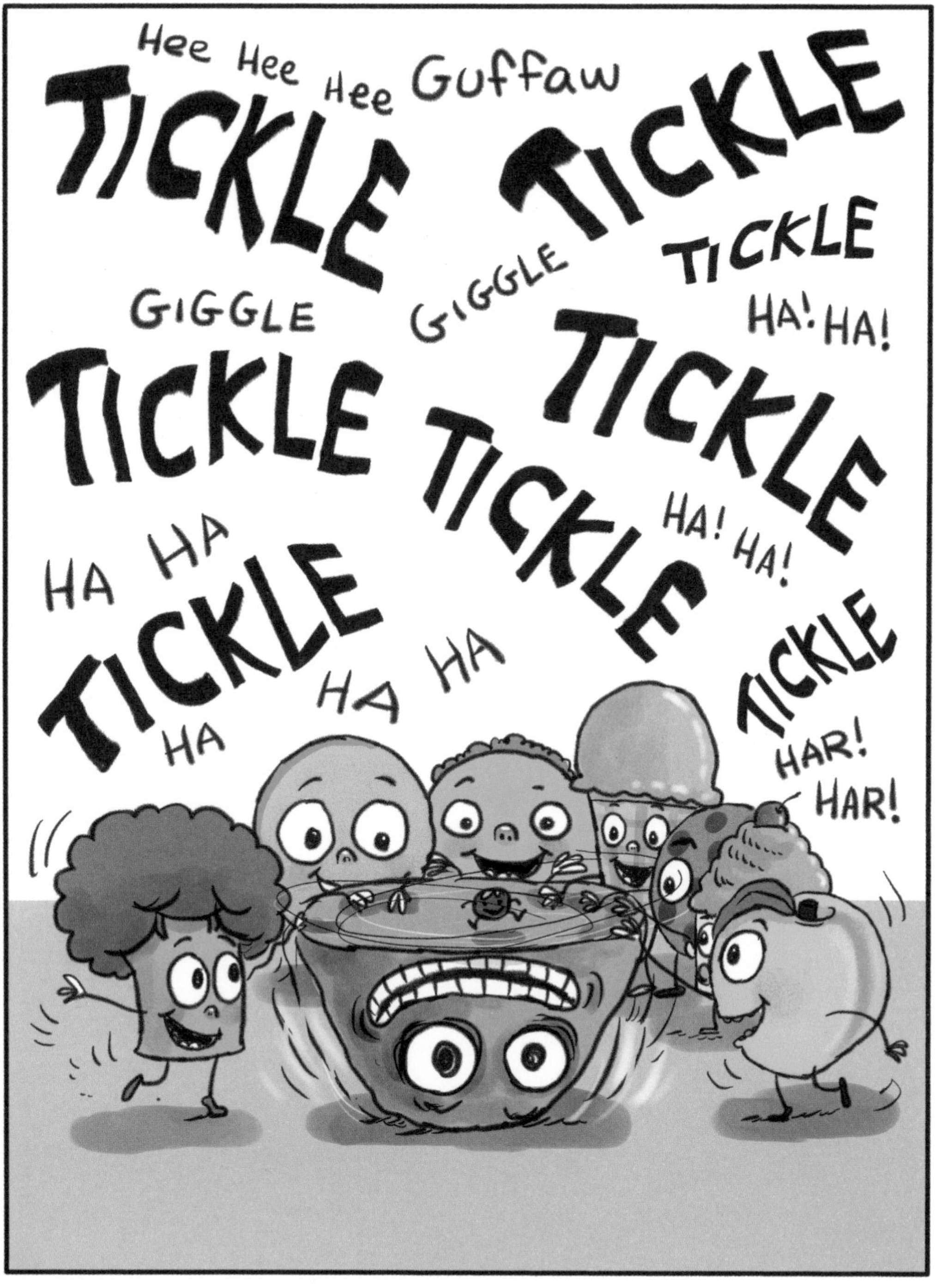
Hee Hee Hee Guffaw
TICKLE
TICKLE
GIGGLE
GIGGLE
TICKLE
HA! HA!
TICKLE
TICKLE
TICKLE
HA HA
HA! HA!
TICKLE
TICKLE
HA HA HA
HA
TICKLE
HAR!
HAR!

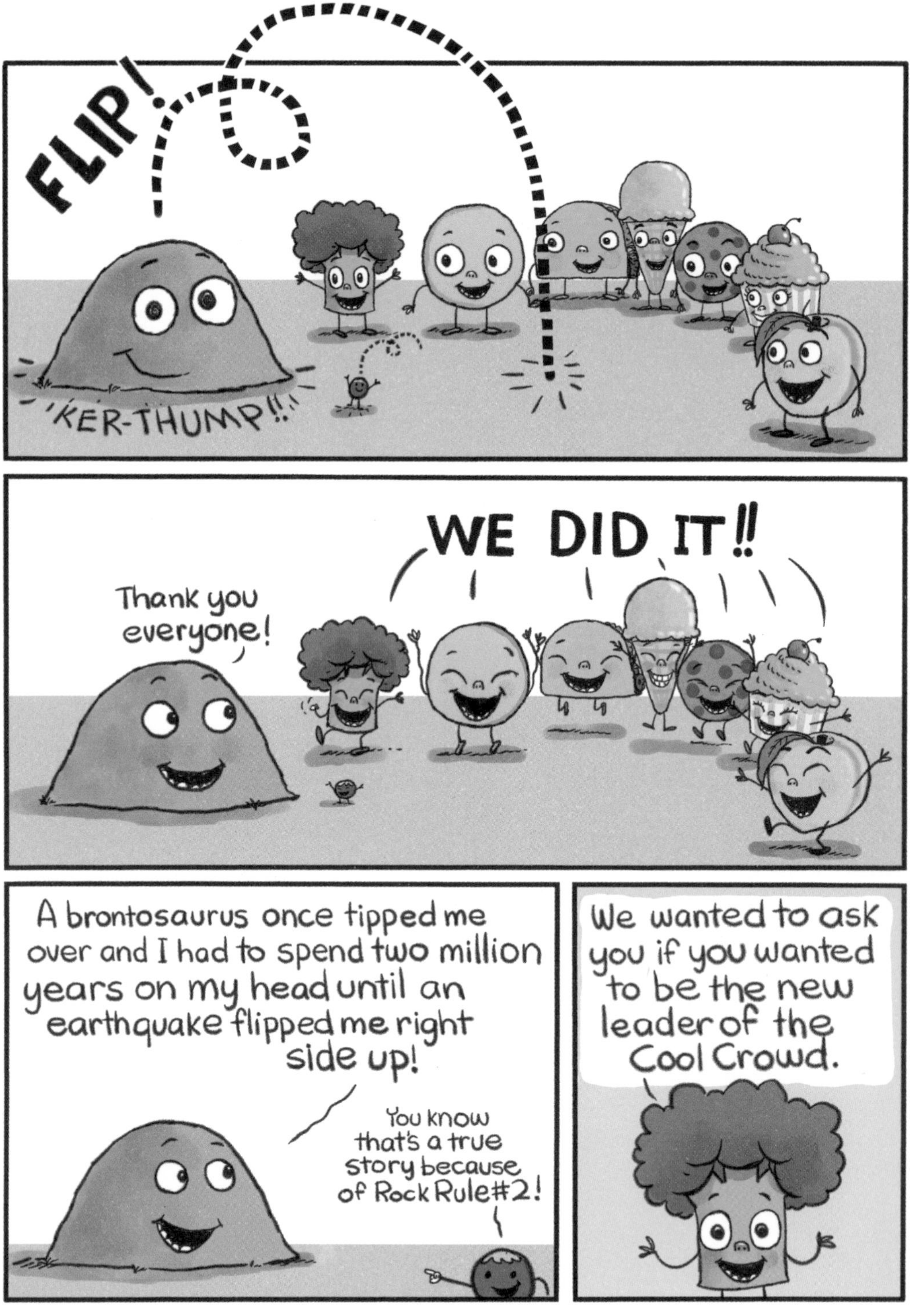
FLIP!
KER-THUMP!!
Thank you everyone!
WE DID IT!!
A brontosaurus once tipped me over and I had to spend two million years on my head until an earthquake flipped me right side up!
You know that's a true story because of Rock Rule #2!
We wanted to ask you if you wanted to be the new leader of the Cool Crowd.

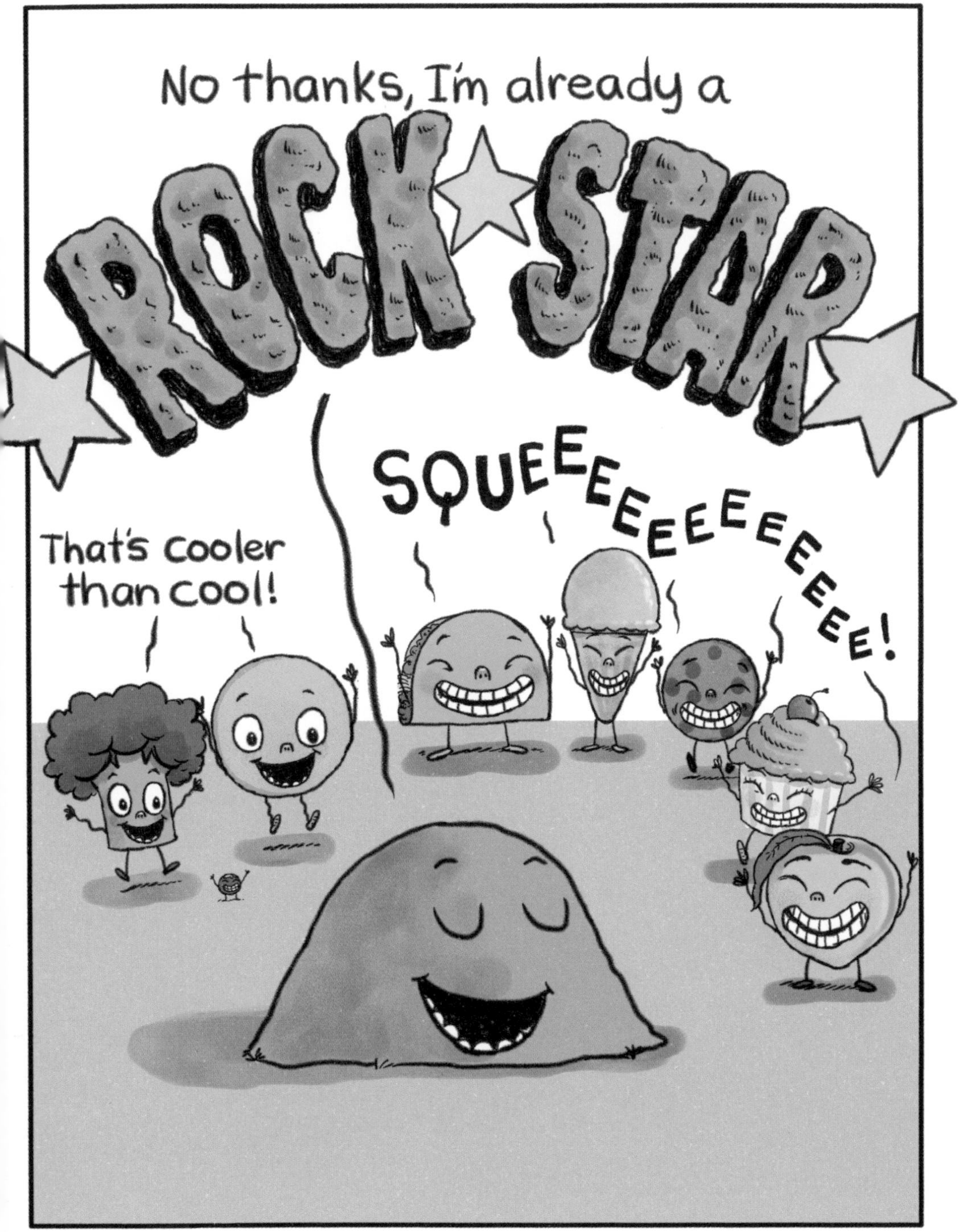
No thanks, I'm already a
ROCK STAR
That's cooler than cool!
SQUEEEEEEEEEEEEEEE!

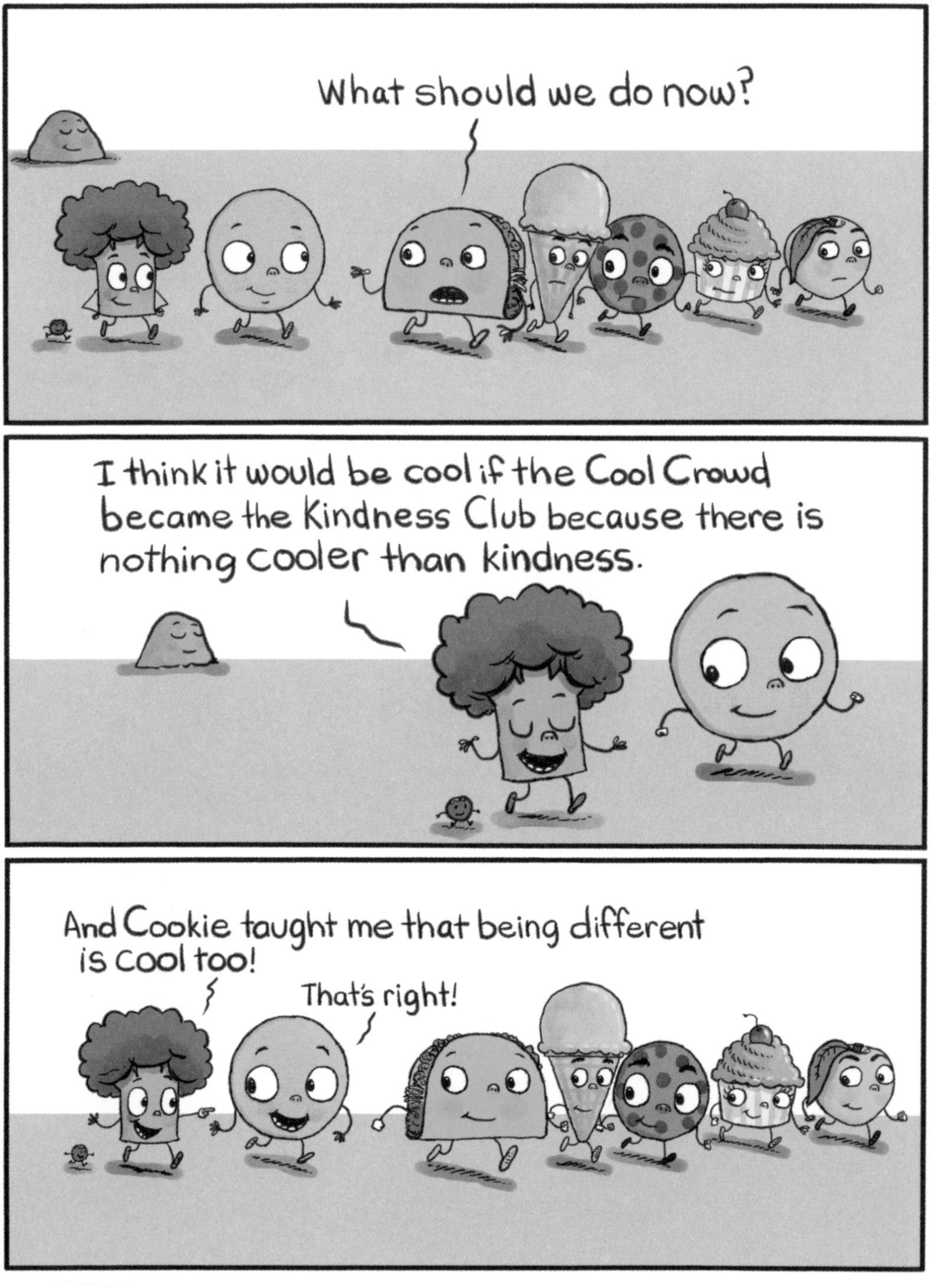
What should we do now?
I think it would be cool if the Cool Crowd became the Kindness Club because there is nothing cooler than kindness.
And Cookie taught me that being different is cool too!
That's right!

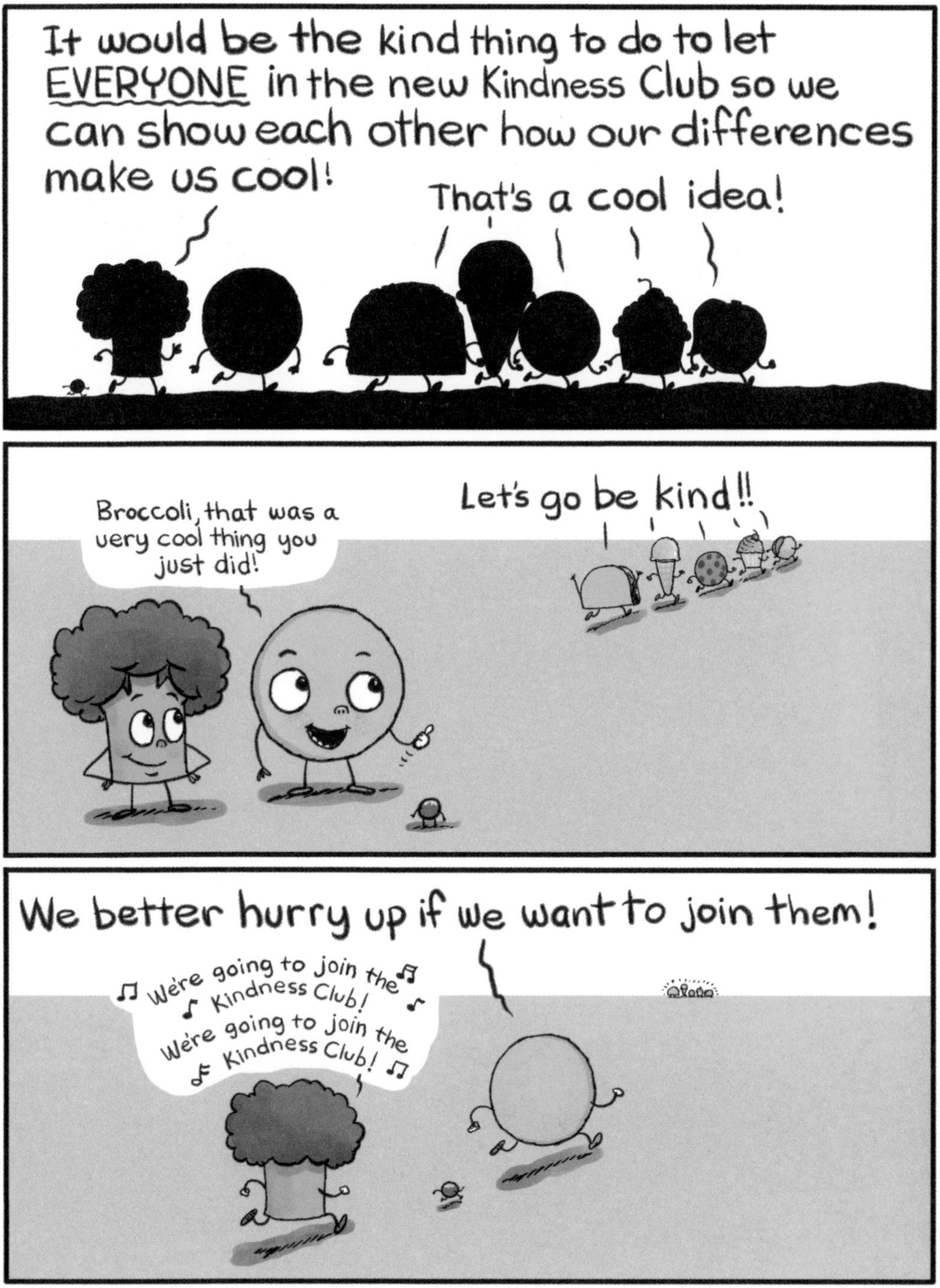
It would be the kind thing to do to let EVERYONE in the new Kindness Club so we can show each other how our differences make us cool!
That's a cool idea!
Broccoli, that was a very cool thing you just did!
Let's go be kind!!
We better hurry up if we want to join them!
We're going to join the Kindness Club! We're going to join the Kindness Club!

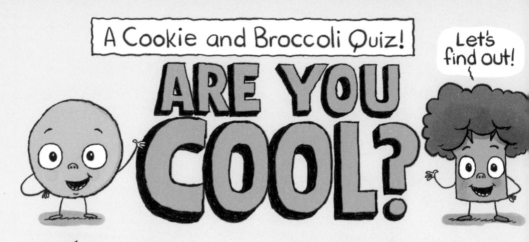

A Cookie and Broccoli Quiz!

ARE YOU COOL?

Let's find out!

1. Are you kind to others?

It's cool to be kind, that's my motto!

YOU'RE COOL!

2. Do you appreciate other people's differences?

I like math!

I like to dance the Hokey Pokey!

YOU'RE COOL!

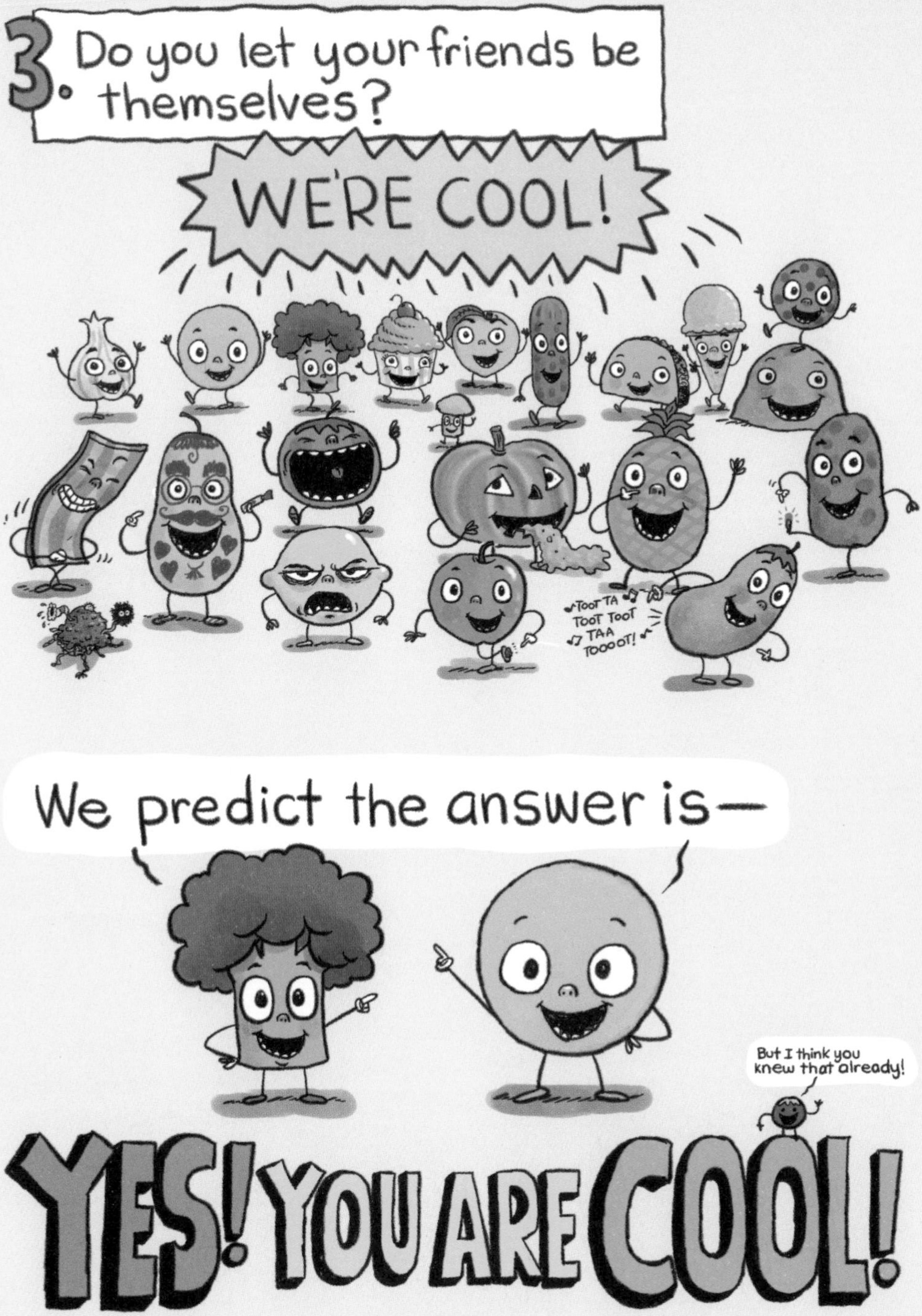
3. Do you let your friends be themselves?
WE'RE COOL!
TOOT TA TOOT TOOT TAA TOOOOT!
We predict the answer is—
But I think you knew that already!
YES! YOU ARE COOL!

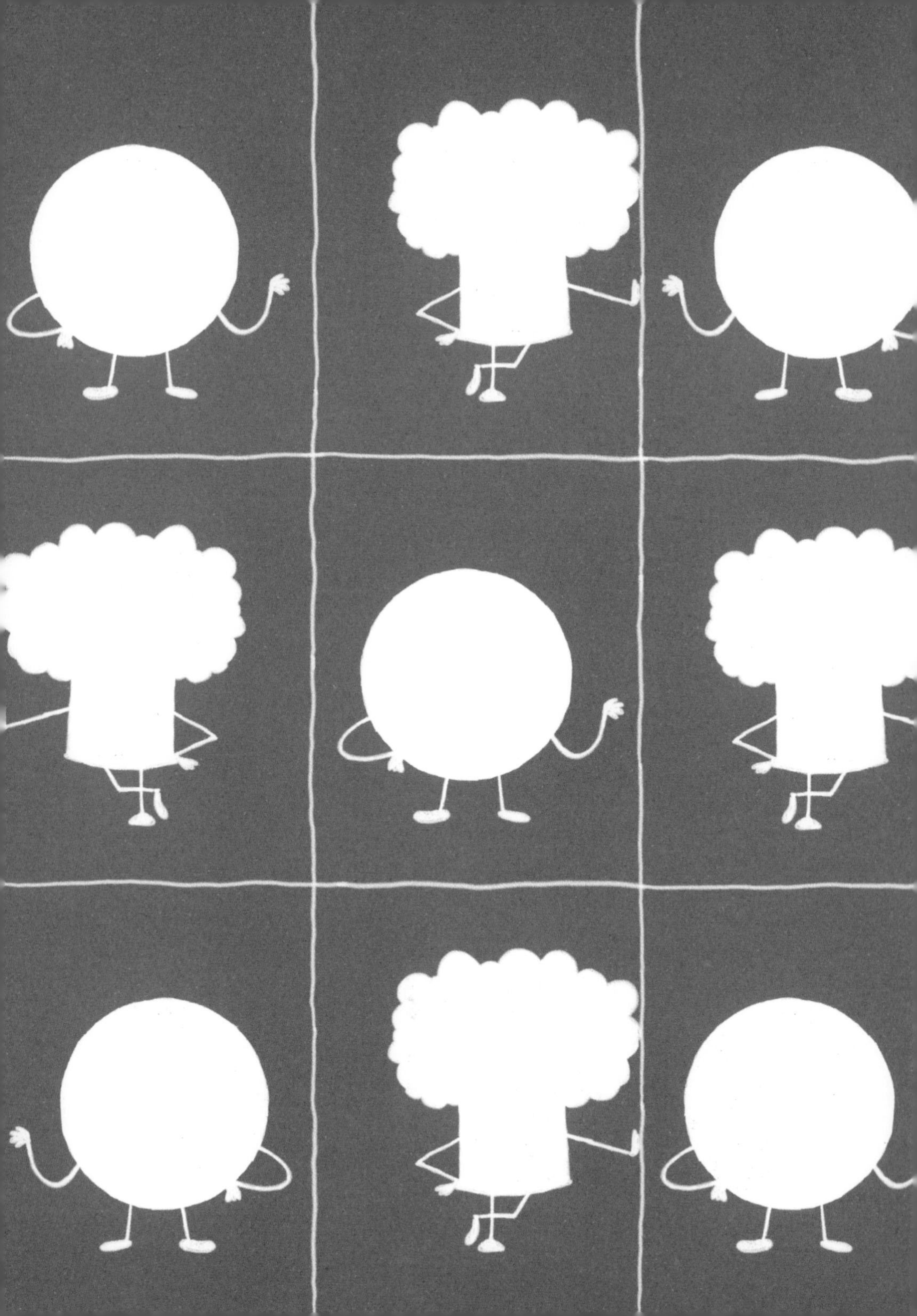

Epilogue

"Epilogue" is a cool word!

I can tell by looking at your face!

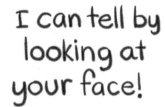

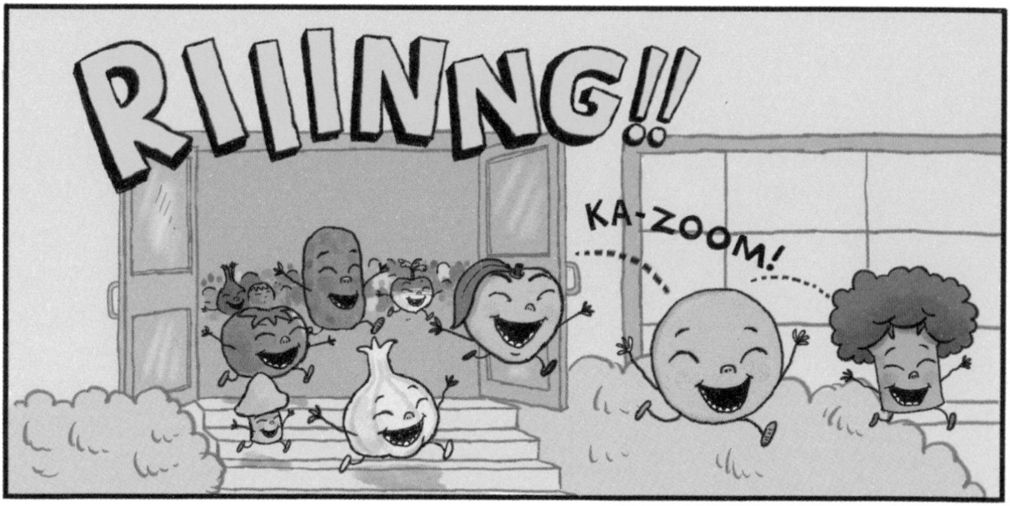
RIIINNG!!
KA-ZOOM!

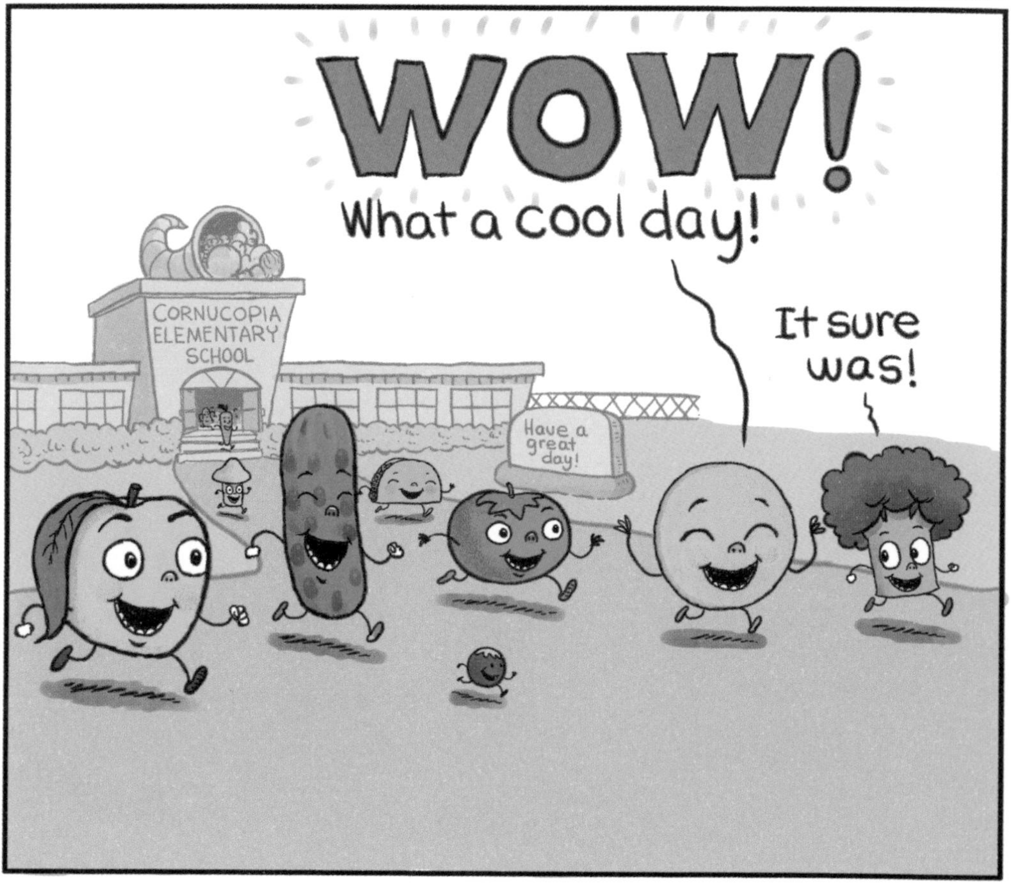
CORNUCOPIA ELEMENTARY SCHOOL
Have a great day!
WOW! What a cool day!
It sure was!

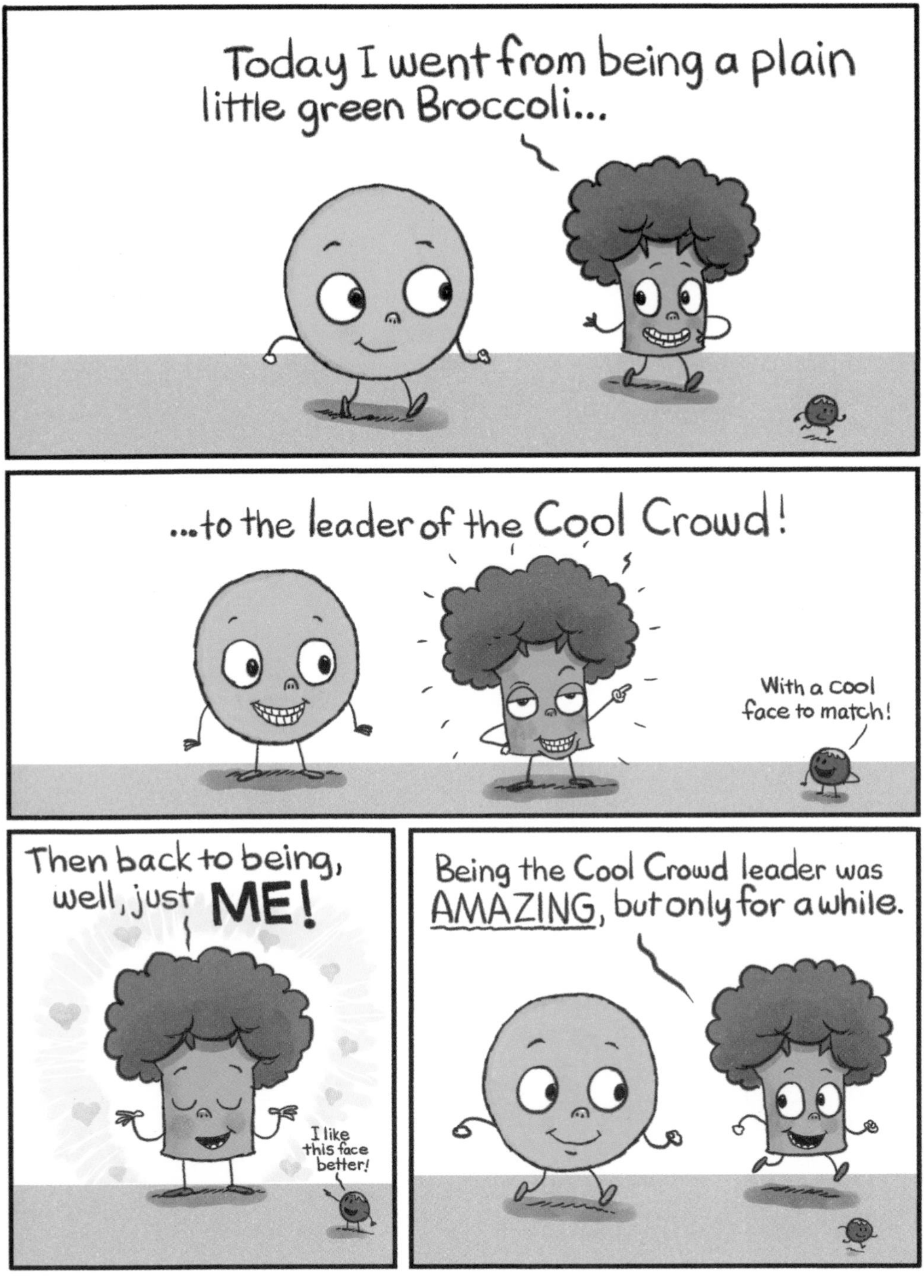
Today I went from being a plain little green Broccoli...
...to the leader of the Cool Crowd!
With a cool face to match!
Then back to being, well, just ME!
I like this face better!
Being the Cool Crowd leader was AMAZING, but only for a while.

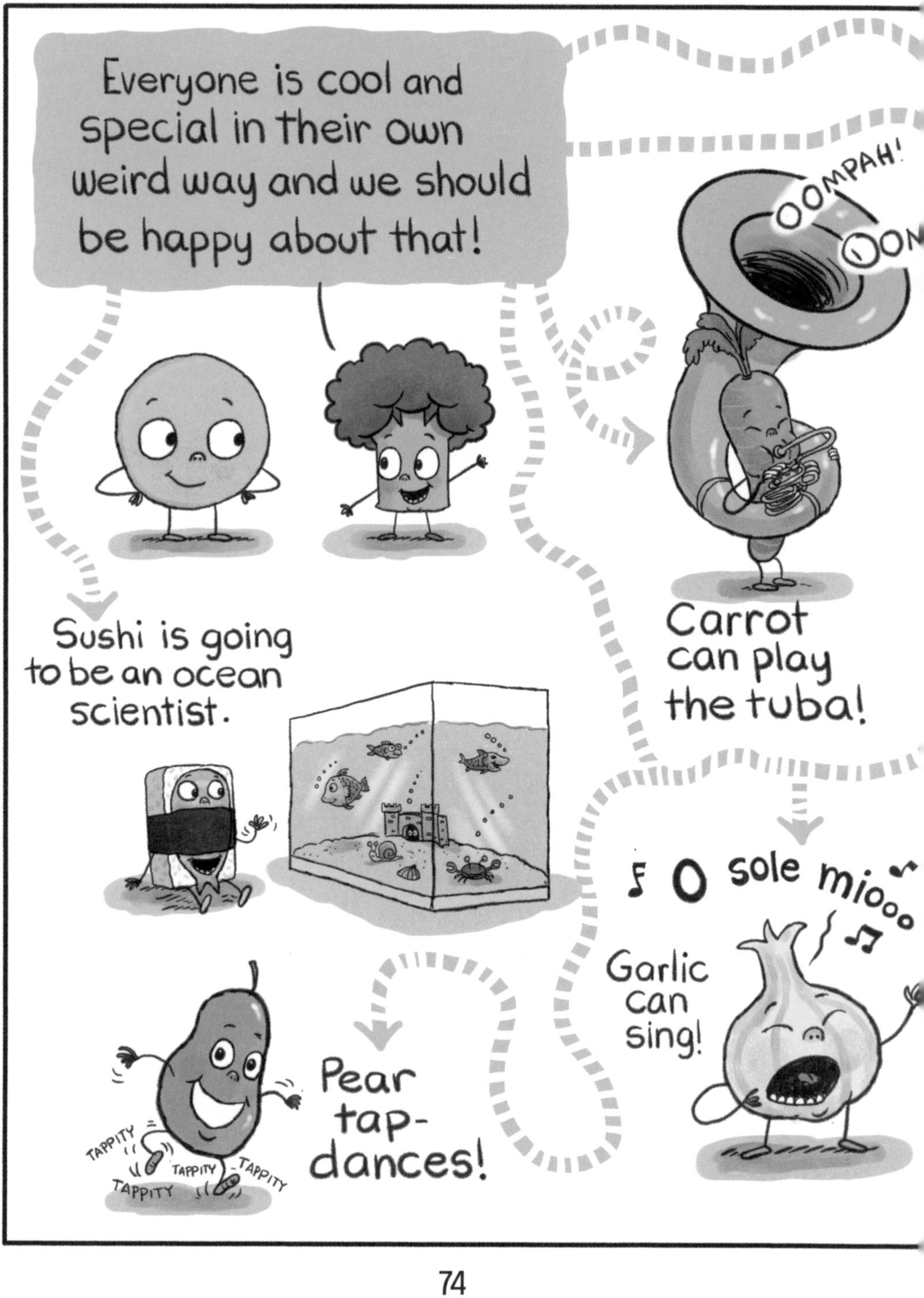
Everyone is cool and special in their own weird way and we should be happy about that!
OOMPAH!
OOM
Carrot can play the tuba!
Sushi is going to be an ocean scientist.
O sole mioooo
Garlic can sing!
TAPPITY
TAPPITY
TAPPITY
TAPPITY
Pear tap-dances!

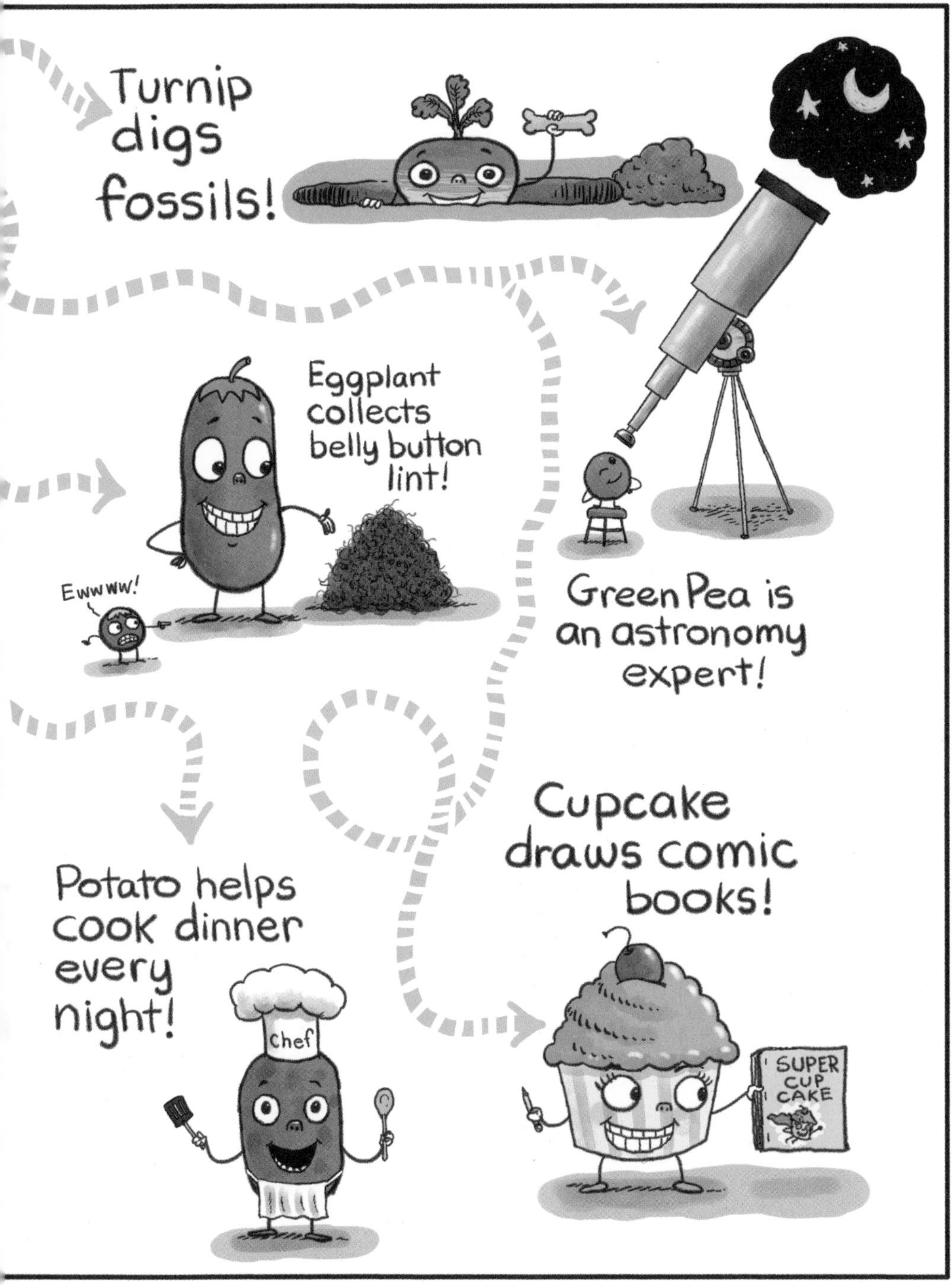
Turnip digs fossils!
Eggplant collects belly button lint!
Ewwww!
Green Pea is an astronomy expert!
Potato helps cook dinner every night!
Chef
Cupcake draws comic books!
SUPER CUP CAKE

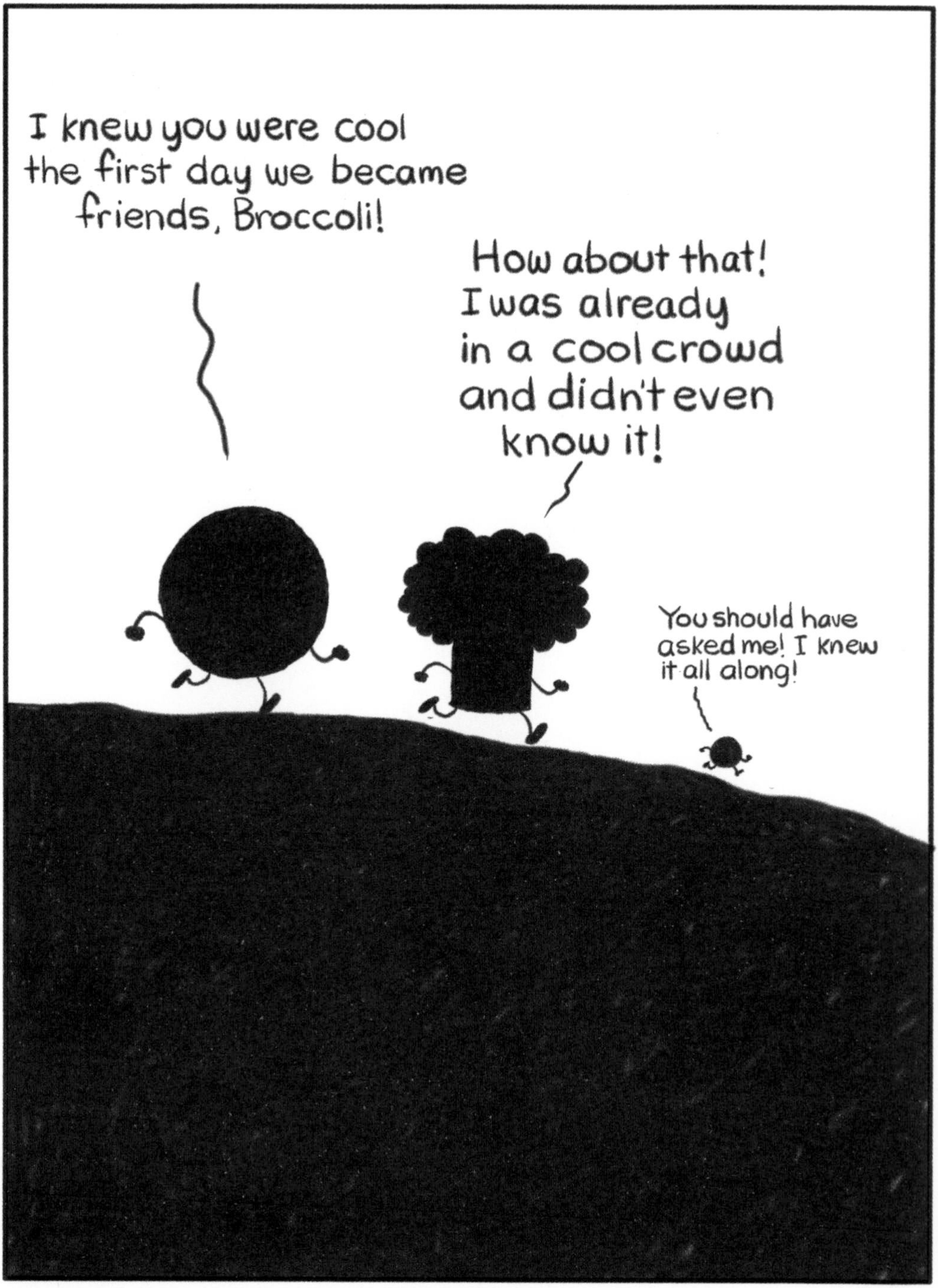
I knew you were cool the first day we became friends, Broccoli!
How about that! I was already in a cool crowd and didn't even know it!
You should have asked me! I knew it all along!

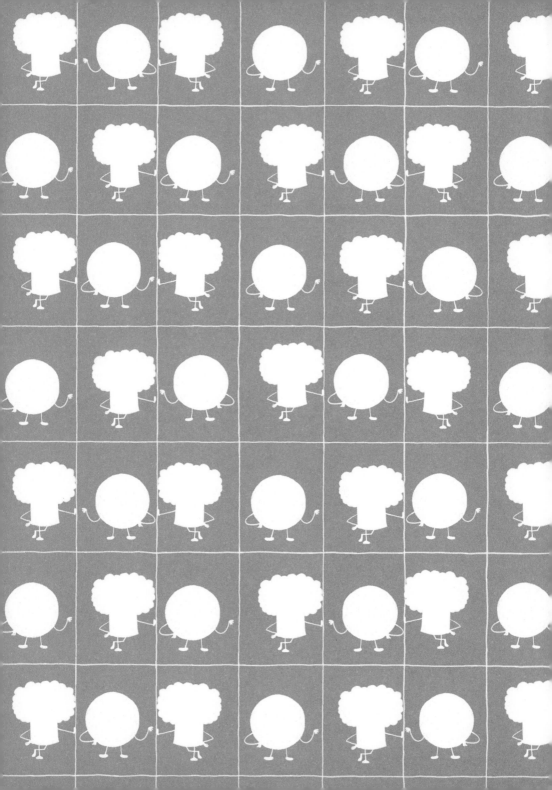